Praise for кiffe кiffe томоrrow

"A confection that is tender, fun[...] [*Kiffe Kiffe*] challenges the conven[...] the suburbs are only dangerous, cri[...] lands where hatred runs deep and ho[...] [...]cent."
—*The New York Times*

"A lighthearted bonbon of a book...Not since director Mathieu Kassovitz's 1995 hit film *Hate* has there been such a compelling portrait of the Parisian suburbs...French reviewers have been quick to compare *Kiffe Kiffe* to *Bridget Jones's Diary* and, given the main character's spunky, slightly self-deprecating attitude, it's easy to see why. But Doria—a volatile mix of adolescent insecurity, misguided bravado and tenderness—has a lot more than cigarettes, calories and snogging on her mind."   —*Newsweek International*

"The surprise publishing hit of 2004 [in France] was not the latest Houellebecq or Beigbeder but a tender and funny first novel by a nineteen-year-old writer of Algerian parentage about her run-down high-rise estate north of Paris. Faïza Guène instantly became 'la Sagan des Cités' or the Brontë of the 'burbs...Full of humanity and wry humour, stuffed with memorable characters...the novel is a kind of French *White Teeth*."

"A Bridget Jones teenager of the projects."

"It's sad, it's funny, it's packed with talent, the author, Faïza Guène, is only nineteen, and we know we're going to be talking about her again soon."

"[Guène] writes like Jamel Debbouze talks. It's a language full of wisecracks and lucidity, of exaggerated numbers delivered without a decoder. Faïza has the gift of observation. And loving life whatever it is."

"With [Doria], you get to see the part of France where the people aren't entirely French, are always living caught between two worlds, now more than ever. And you begin to feel—like her—filled with democratic spirit."

kiffe kiffe tomorrow

Kiffe Kiffe Tomorrow

Faïza Guène

A HARVEST ORIGINAL/HARCOURT, INC.
Orlando   Austin
New York   San Diego
Toronto   London

www.HarcourtBooks.com

This is a translation of *Kiffe kiffe demain*,
first published by Hachette Littératures in 2004.

This translation is an edited version of Sarah Adams's translation,
published by Chatto & Windus in the United Kingdom.

Library of Congress Cataloging-in-Publication Data
Guène, Faïza.
[Kiffe kiffe demain. English]
Kiffe kiffe tomorrow/Faïza Guène.
p. cm.
"A Harvest Original."
I. Title.
PQ3989.3.G84K5413   2006
843'.92—dc22   2005030456
ISBN-13: 978-0-15-603048-9   ISBN-10: 0-15-603048-9

Text set in Fournier
Designed by Kaelin Chappell Broaddus

Printed in the United States of America
First edition

K J I H G F E D C B A

For my mother and my father

bled: (1) a village; (2) a godforsaken place, the middle of nowhere, a wasteland; (3) a hole or dump; (4) (North African) countryside, the interior / мασhreb: North Africa / mekтoub: lit. "it is written," destiny / inshallah: lit. "if Allah wills," god willing / hchouma: shame, disgrace, indecency / kif-kif: same old, same old; it's all the same / kiffeɾ: to be really crazy about something

It's Monday and, like every Monday, I went over to Madame Burlaud's. Mme Burlaud is old, she's ugly, and she stinks like RID antilice shampoo. She's harmless, but sometimes she worries me. Today she took a whole bunch of weird pictures out of her bottom drawer. They were these huge blobs that looked like dried vomit. She asked me what they made me think about. When I told her she stared at me with her eyes all bugged out, shaking her head like those little toy dogs in the backs of cars.

It was school that sent me up to see her. The teachers, in between strikes for once, figured I'd better see somebody because I seemed shut down or closed off or something...Maybe they're right. I don't give a shit. I go. It's covered by welfare.

I guess I've been like this since my dad left. He went a way long way away, back to Morocco to marry another woman, who must be younger and more fertile than my mom. After me, Mom couldn't have any more children. But it wasn't like she didn't try. She tried for a really long time. When I think of all the girls who get pregnant their first time, not even on purpose...Dad, he wanted a son. For his pride, his reputation, the family honor, and I'm sure lots of other stupid reasons. But he only got one kid and it was a girl. Me. You could say I didn't exactly meet customer specifications. Trouble is, it's not like at the supermarket: There's no customer-satisfaction guarantee. So one day the Beard must have realized there was no point trying anymore with my mom and he took off. Just like that, no warning. All I remember is that I was watching an episode from the fourth season of *The X-Files* that I'd rented from the video store on the corner. The door banged shut. From the window, I saw a gray taxi pulling away. That's all. It's been over six months. That peasant woman he married is probably pregnant by now. And I know exactly how it will all go down: Seven days after the birth they'll hold the baptism ceremony and invite the whole village. A band of old sheiks carting their camel-hide drums will come over just for the big event. It's going to cost him a real fortune—all his pension from the Renault factory. And then they'll slit the throat of a giant sheep to give the baby its first name. It'll be Mohammed. Ten to one.

When Mme Burlaud asks me if I miss my dad, I say "no," but she doesn't believe me. She's pretty smart like that, for a chick. Whatever, it's no big deal, my mom's here. Well, she's here physically. Because in her head, she's somewhere else. Somewhere even farther away than my father.

Ramadan started a little over a week ago. I made Mom sign a form saying why I wouldn't be eating in the cafeteria. When I gave it to the principal, he asked if I was trying to put one over on him. His name is Monsieur Loiseau. He's fat, he's stupid, he smokes a pipe, and when he opens his mouth it reeks of cheap wine. At the end of the day, his big sister picks him up out front of school in a red hatchback. So when he wants to play the big boss, he's got a real credibility problem.

Anyway, M. Loiseau asked me if I was taking him for a ride because he thought I'd forged my mom's name on the paper. He's an idiot. If I'd wanted to fake a signature, I'd have made it look like a real one. On this thing Mom just made a kind of squiggly line. She's not used to holding a pen. The jerk didn't even think about that, didn't even ask himself why her signature might be weird. He's one of those people who think illiteracy is like AIDS. It only exists in Africa.

Not very long ago Mom started working. She cleans rooms at the Formula 1 Motel in Bagnolet while she's waiting to find something else, soon I hope. Sometimes, when she gets home late at night, she cries. She says it's from feeling so tired. She struggles even harder during Ramadan, because when it's time to break the fast, around 5:30 P.M., she's still at work. So if she wants to eat, she has to hide some dates in her smock. She even sewed an inside pocket so she can be sly about it, because if her boss saw her he'd be totally pissed.

Everyone calls her "Fatma" at the Formula 1. They shout at her all the time, and they keep a close watch on her to make sure she doesn't steal anything from the rooms.

Of course, Mom's name isn't Fatma, it's Yasmina. It must really give Monsieur Winner a charge to call all the Arabs "Fatma," all the blacks "Mamadou," and all the Chinese "Ping-Pong." Pretty freaking lame.

M. Winner is Mom's supervisor. He's from Alsace. Sometimes I wish he'd waste away at the bottom of a deep, dark basement, getting eaten alive by rats. When I say that, Mom gives me shit. She says it's not good to wish death on anybody, not even your worst enemy. One day he insulted her and when she got home she cried like crazy. Last time I saw someone crying like that was when Myriam peed her pants in skiing class. That bastard Winner thought Mom was disrespecting him because, with her accent, she pronounced his name "Weener."

since the old man split we've had a whole parade of social workers coming to the apartment. Can't remember the new one's name, but it's something like Dubois or Dupont or Dupré, a name that tells you she's from somewhere, from a real family line or something. I think she's stupid, and she smiles all the time for no good reason. Even when it's clearly not the right time. It's like the crazy woman feels the need to be happy for other people because they aren't happy for themselves. Once, she asked if I wanted us to be friends. Like a little brat I told her I didn't see that happening. But I guess I messed up, because the look my mother gave me cut me in half. She was probably

scared social services would cut off our benefits if I
didn't make nice with their stupid social worker.

Before Mme DuThingamajig, it was a man...
Yeah, she took over from this guy who looked like
Laurent Cabrol, the one who hosted *Heroes' Night* on
TF1 on Friday nights. Shame it's not on anymore.
Now Laurent Cabrol's in the bottom right-hand corner of *TV Mag*, page 30, wearing a yellow and black
striped rugby shirt, advertising central heating. Anyway, this social worker was his spitting image. Total
opposite of Mme DuWhatsit. He never cracked a
joke, he never smiled, and he dressed like Professor
Calculus in *The Adventures of Tintin*. Once, he told
my mom that in ten years on this job, this was the first
time he'd seen "people like you with only one child."
He was thinking "Arabs," but he didn't say so. Coming to our place was like an exotic experience for him.
He kept giving weird looks to all the knick-knacks
around the house, the ones my mom brought over
from Morocco after she got married. And since we
wear *babouches* at home, he'd take off his shoes when
he walked in, trying to do the right thing. Except he
had alien feet. His second toe was at least ten times
longer than his big toe. It looked like he was giving us

the finger through his socks. And then there was the stench. The whole time he played the sweet, compassionate type, but it was all a front. He didn't give a shit about us. Besides, he quit. Seems he moved to the countryside. Remade himself into a cheese-maker, for all I know. He drives around the little villages of dear old la belle France in his sky blue van on Sunday mornings after Mass, selling rye bread, old-fashioned Roquefort cheese, and *saucisson sec*.

Even if I think Mme DuSomethingorother's a fool too, at least she does a better job of playing social worker to the local poor. She really makes out like she gives a damn about our lives. Sometimes, you'd almost believe her. She fires questions at me in this high-pitched voice. The other day she wanted to know the last book I'd read. I just shrugged so she'd think the answer was "nothing." But, really, I've just finished this thing called *The Sand Child* by Tahar Ben Jelloun. It tells all about a little girl who was raised as a boy because she was the eighth daughter in the family and her father wanted a son. Back when the book is set, there wasn't any ultrasound or contraception. It was no refunds, no exchanges.

———

What a shitty destiny. Fate is all trial and misery and you can't do anything about it. Basically no matter what you do you'll always get screwed over. My mom says my dad walked out on us because it was written that way. Around here, we call it *mektoub*. It's like a film script and we're the actors. Trouble is, our scriptwriter's got no talent. And he's never heard of happily ever after.

disolutionnment

MY mom always dreamed France was like in those black-and-white films from the sixties. The ones where the handsome actor's always telling his woman so many pretty lies, a cigarette dangling from his lips. Back in Morocco, my mom and her cousin Bouchra found a way to pick up French channels with this antenna they rigged up from a stainless-steel couscous maker. So when she and my dad arrived in Livry-Gargan, just north of Paris, in February 1984, she thought they must have taken the wrong boat and ended up in the wrong country. She told me that when she walked into this tiny two-room apartment the first thing she did was throw up. I'm not sure if it was seasickness or a sixth sense warning her about her future in this *bled*.

The last time we went back to Morocco, I was wild-eyed and dazed. I remember these old, tattooed women coming over and sitting next to Mom at the weddings and baptisms and circumcision ceremonies.

"You know, Yasmina, your girl is getting to be a woman, you have to think about finding her a boy from a good family. Do you know Rachid? That young man who's a welder..."

Stupid old bags. I know exactly who they're talking about. Everyone calls him "Mule-head Rachid." Even the six-year-olds make fun of him to his face. Not to mention he's missing four teeth, he can't read at all, he's cross-eyed, and he stinks like piss. Over there, it's enough that you have even the smallest little bumps for breasts, you know to shut up when you're told to, you know how to bake decent bread, and bam, you're all ready for marriage. Anyway, I don't think we're ever going back to Morocco. We can't afford it for one thing, and my mom says it would be too humiliating. People would point at her and whisper. She thinks what happened is all her fault. To me there are only two guilty parties in this story: my dad and fate.

We worry about the future but there's no point. For all we know we might not even have one. You could die in ten days, or tomorrow, or suddenly, right over there, right now. It's the kind of thing that doesn't exactly make an appointment. There's no advance notice, no final warning. Not like when your electricity bill payment is overdue. That's how it was for Monsieur Rodriguez, my neighbor from the eleventh floor, the one who fought in the war for real. He died not long ago. Sure, OK, he was old, but, still, no one expected it.

Sometimes I think about death. I even dream about it. One night I was at my own funeral. Hardly anyone there. Just my mom; Mme Burlaud; Carla, the Portuguese lady who cleans the elevators in our tower; Leonardo DiCaprio from *Titanic;* and my friend Sarah, who moved to that suburb Trappes, south of Paris, when I was twelve. My dad wasn't there. He must have been busy with his peasant woman who was pregnant with his Momo-to-be, while I was, well, dead. It's disgusting. I'll bet you his son's going to be stupid, even slower than Rachid the welder. I hope he'll limp, have problems with his eyesight, and when he hits puberty he'll suffer from the worst possible acne. He won't be able to get ahold of any Clearasil for his zits in their crappy, middle-of-nowhere *bled*. Except maybe on the black market, if he knows how to work the system. Whichever way you look at it, he'll turn out to be a loser. In this family, being a stupid bastard is passed down from father to son. At sixteen, he'll be selling potatoes and turnips at the market. And on his trip home every day, riding his black mule, he'll tell himself: "I am one glamorous guy."

Someday I'd like to work at something glamorous myself, but I don't know what exactly... The trouble is, I'm no good at school. Completely useless. The only class I even scrape by in is Art and Design. That's fine and all, but I don't think gluing leaves on drawing paper is going to be a big help for my future. Whatever, I just don't want to end up behind a fast-food register, smiling all the time and asking customers: "Would you like a drink? Regular or super-

sized? For here or to go? For or against abortion?"
And getting torn up by my supervisor if I serve a customer too many fries because he smiled at me...No
lie, that guy could have been the man of my dreams.
I would have given him a discount on his McMeal,
he'd have taken me to eat at a swank steakhouse, asked
me to marry him, and we'd have lived happily ever
after in his five-room to-die-for apartment.

welfare
charity stores
loans/borrowing

our welfare stamps finally came. Just in time—now I won't have to go to the big charity store in the middle of town. That place is too much to bear. Once, me and my mom ran into Nacéra the witch near the main entrance. She's this woman we've known since forever. Mom borrows money from her when we're full out broke. I hate her. She only remembers we owe her cash when there are tons of people around, always just to fuck with my mom's image. So we run into Nacéra at the main entrance. Mom's squirming, but this other woman, she's just over the moon.

"So, Yasmina, you've come to the goodwill to...
pick something up?"

"Yes..."

"And I've come to...give!"

"May God reward you..."

Yeah right. I hope God rewards her with nothing
except the nastiness of being an ugly old woman. In
the end, we went home without getting anything, because Mom didn't want to chance picking clothes that
belonged to the witch. It would just give her another
excuse to open her big mouth, like, "Oh, that skirt
you're wearing used to be mine..." I was proud of
my mom. That's real dignity—the kind of thing you
don't learn at school.

Speaking of school, I've got to do a homework as-
signment for civics, all about the idea of respect.
Monsieur Werbert gave it to us. He's an OK teacher
and he's nice, but I don't really like him talking to me
too much, because I get the idea he feels sorry for me
or something and I hate that. It's like at the charity
store, when Mom asks the old woman for a plastic
bag to put our sweaters in and she looks at us all
misty-eyed. Every time, we just want to give her

back her sweaters and get the hell out of there. With
M. Werbert it's the same. He makes out that he's
some kind of prophet of the people. He keeps telling
me I can have a meeting with him, if I ever need
one... But it's just so he can feel good about himself
and tell his friends in some hip Paris bar how hard it
is teaching at-risk youth in the ghetto suburbs. Yuck.

So what could I say about respect? The teachers
don't give a shit about our homework. I'm sure they
don't even read any of it. They just stick on a random
grade, rearrange the papers, and go back to sitting
on their leather couches between their two kids—
Pamela, ten, who's playing with Dishwasher Barbie,
and Brandon, twelve, who's busy eating his own snot.
And don't forget Marie-Hélène, who orders takeout
because she's too lazy to cook dinner, and who's reading an article in *Woman Today* about waxing your
legs. Now that's a good example of disrespect. Waxing hurts, and if you hurt somebody it shows a lack of
respect.

Whatever, I want to drop out. I've had enough of
school. It gets on my nerves and I don't talk to anybody. Really, there are only two people I can talk to
for real anywhere. Mme Burlaud and Hamoudi, one

of the older guys in the complex. He's probably about twenty-eight, he spends all day every day hanging around all the lobbies in the neighborhood towers, and, like he's always telling me, he's known me since I was "no bigger than a block of hash."

Hamoudi spends most of his time smoking a lot of spliffs. He's always high and I think maybe that's why I like him. The two of us, we don't like our reality. Sometimes when I get back from running errands, he stops me in the hall to talk about stuff. "Just five minutes," he says, and then we talk for an hour or two. Well, it's mostly him. A lot of times he recites for me these poems by Arthur Rimbaud. At least the little he can remember, because the hash can really fuck with your memory. But when he says them to me in his accent with those street gangster moves, even if I don't catch all the meaning, it seems beautiful to me.

It's way too bad he didn't keep up with school. It's because of prison. He told me that he and his friends got mixed up in some kind of bad business, but he won't tell me what—he says "it's not for kids your age." When he got out, he dropped everything even though he was pretty far along with his studies. At least as far as the bac, the college entrance tests. So when I see the police patting Hamoudi down near our lobby, when I hear them calling him stuff like "little bastard," or "piece of trash," I tell myself that these guys, they don't know shit about poetry. If Hamoudi were a little older, I'd have liked him for my dad. When he found out what happened to us, he talked to me for the longest time. Rolling his billionth joint, he said: "Family, that's the most sacred thing." He should know: He has eight brothers and sisters and almost all of them are married. But Hamoudi says he doesn't give a fuck about marriage, that there's no point, that it's just something else to hold you back, like we don't have enough of that already. He's right. Except me, I don't really have a family anymore. We're just a half family now.

I was feeling kind of bored, so I decided to hop a ride on the metro. I didn't know where I was going, but the metro takes my mind off stuff. You see so many different kinds of people, it's kind of a riot. I did the whole of Line 5, end to end.

At one of the early stops, this Romanian guy with an old, fake leather jacket and a gray hat got in. He had an accordion, all worn out, with dust on the keys he never uses. He played bits of old tunes, like the kind you hear in artsy films or on those mind-numbing documentaries that run on late-night TV. It was cool because he really made the trip more fun. I saw even the most uptight old people in the car tapping their toes on the sly. And the gypsy guy bobbed his head with each movement of his instrument, and when he smiled he flashed all his teeth, at least the ones that were still left. His whole face was straight out of a cartoon, kind of like the cat in *Alice in Wonderland*.

I sat there imagining that he lived in a caravan, the descendant of a great dynasty of nomads who'd crossed land after land after land; that he lived in a makeshift camp on a patch of wasteland outside Paris; that he had a pretty wife named Lucia (like the mozzarella brand) with long black hair that falls down her back in perfect curls. These two, they were married on a wide-open beach on the Spanish coast, around a huge fire with giant red flames that danced way into the middle of the night. It had to have happened that way. Anyway, each time he switched cars I followed him, so I could get the most out of his accordion poetry. But in the end, talk about dying of shame. He headed over to me, holding out his McDonald's paper cup with loose change in it, and, well, basically I didn't have anything to give him. So I played the meanest kind of trick, the kind stingy bastards do all the time. As soon as the good man got next to me, I looked the other way, as in "I'm watching what's going down on the opposite platform." Except, big surprise, there was nothing going down on the opposite platform.

If I win the lottery on Wednesday, I'll give him a swank caravan all tricked out, it'll be the best-looking one on the campsite. It'll look just like the ones you can win in the showcase showdown on *The Price Is Right*.

Then I'd buy myself some new mittens for winter, with no holes, because with mine cold air just comes right in. On my left mitten, there's a big hole right over the middle finger. I just know one of these days that's going to cause me big problems.

Next, I'd take Mom to get a manicure, because that's what she was talking about last time with that social worker Mme DuThing, and my mother didn't even know what it was. She looked at her own nails, all completely torn up from those made-in-Chernobyl cleaning products, and compared them with Mme DuThingamajig's. That fool social worker was showing off because her nails were super clean, super shaped, super polished. She even rubbed the corner of her eye with her little finger, her mouth ever so slightly open, the way girls on TV put on mascara. All that just to gloat, to put her perfect nails all up in my mom's face, my mom who didn't even know what a manicure was. I wanted to rip them out one by one.

At the end of the line, when I was getting out of the metro, I passed two Pakistani guys selling hot chestnuts and roasted peanuts. They kept saying the same thing, over and over again: "Hot chestnuts and roasted peanuts to warm you up!" They said it together, all musical, sang it almost, with their Pakistani accents. I couldn't get those words out of my head, and that evening, when I got back home, I ended up singing it while I was cooking Mom her rice.

fridαy. Mom and me, we're invited over to Aunt Zohra's to eat some couscous. We took the earliest possible train so we could spend the whole day at her place. It's been forever since anyone invited us somewhere.

Aunt Zohra isn't my real aunt, but seeing as she's known Mom for a very long time, I call her that just out of habit. Before, they always used to do their sewing together. Then Aunt Zohra moved to Mantes-la-Jolie, which is sort of northeast of Paris, on the way to Rouen. Mom told me she signed up for sewing lessons because it was practically all Maghrebian women and those Wednesday afternoon sessions with all those women at their eighties-style Singer sewing machines reminded her a little of the *bled*.

Aunt Zohra, she's got big green eyes and she laughs all the time. She's Western Algerian, from a region called Tlemcen. She's got a funny story, because she was born on July 5, 1962, the very day Algeria won its independence. For so many years in her village she was like the little child who meant freedom. She was like a baby good-luck charm, and that's why they called her Zohra. It means *luck* in Arabic.

I like her a lot, because she's a real woman. A strong woman. Her husband retired from civil service and married a second wife back in the old country, so he spends six months over there and six months in France. Is this a trend, or what? All these men, it's like they get to be retirement age and they want to totally start their lives over and marry a fresh young woman. The difference is, Aunt Zohra's husband knew how to hit the right balance, rein himself in. He does it part-time...

It doesn't seem to bother Zohra one bit seeing her husband six months out of twelve. She says she's just fine without him, that she can keep herself happy. And then, one time, she laughed and told Mom that a man his age, he doesn't really serve her purposes anyway. That didn't really click at first. Then I kind of got the picture.

I hung out a little with Aunt Zohra's sons, Réda, Hamza, and Youssef. They spent almost the whole time playing video games. These were the kind of games you see in TV reports on "youth and violence." The idea was to break car-speed records while knocking over as many pedestrians as possible, with bonus points if they were kids or old ladies...I've known these boys since we were little, but I don't really talk to them anymore. So it was a little tense, no one really knew what to say. They made so much fun of me for that. They kept comparing me to Bernardo in *Zorro*, the short guy who looked like a dumbass and who warns Zorro of danger through a system of gestures. He was mute, poor guy.

At one point, I caught the end of a conversation about my dad between Mom and Aunt Zohra. Mom was telling her he wouldn't go to heaven because of what he'd done to his daughter. The way I see it, he won't be going because of what he's done to Mom. Heaven's bouncer just won't let him in. He'll send him packing, straight out. And you know, it bugs me

they're still talking about him. He's not here anymore. The only thing to do is forget about him.

Aunt Zohra's couscous is so special, and what
really makes it are the chickpeas and the very gentle
way she prepares her semolina grains. Aunt Zohra
cracks me up. She's been in France for more than
twenty years and she still talks like she stepped off the
plane at Orly a week ago.

Once, a while ago, she was telling Mom how she'd
signed Hamza up for "carrots." Mom didn't have a
clue what she was talking about. But a few days later,
back home, she started giggling to herself. She suddenly realized that Aunt Zohra meant to say she'd
signed Hamza up for karate...Even Aunt Zohra's
sons tease her. They say she does remixes of Molière's
language. They've tagged her "DJ Zozo."

At the end of the day, Youssef drove us back. He
put on some rap and nobody said a single word the
whole way. I could see that Mom was thinking about
something. She had her face turned to the window,
staring into space. Whenever we were stopped, she
would just look blankly at the red light. Her head
must still be somewhere else.

Youssef drives fast, he's tall, and he's very good

looking. When we were little, we went to the same elementary school and he always stood up for me because I didn't have a brother and he was "a big fifth
grader." I remember we did some campaign together
called "A Grain of Rice Can Save a Life," back in the
nineties when there was the famine in Somalia. He
got me to believe the slogan was serious truth, like
for every grain of rice we sent over we really saved
one life. So when Mom bought me a bag of rice that
weighed five hundred grams, I was all proud of sav-
ing so many lives. That would have been enough, but
I even wanted to count each grain of rice in the package so I could be totally sure there would be a huge
number of Somalians who wouldn't die of hunger,
thanks to me. Thought I was Wonder Woman. But
Youssef was lying to me all along. I'm still pissed at
him...Now that I think about it, I never did hear if
my bag of rice arrived safe and sound.

When we got to our building, Mom thanked Youssef
and he left. You could say the super of our development doesn't give a shit about our towers. Luckily
Carla, the Portuguese cleaning lady, gives them a

quick once-over from time to time. But when she doesn't come, they stay disgusting for weeks on end, and that's how they've been lately. There's been piss and globs of spit in the elevator. It stank, but we were all just happy it was working. It's lucky we know which buttons are for which floors, because the display panel's all scratched and melted. Must have been burned with a cigarette lighter.

Apparently, the super's racist. Hamoudi told me. Me, I wouldn't know, seeing as I've never spoken to him. He kind of scares me. He's always frowning so he's got two lines sticking up in the middle of his forehead, like the number eleven.

Hamoudi told me how back in the day, before this guy was our super, he fought in the war in Aunt Zohra's country, in Algeria. Maybe that's why he hasn't got any earlobes and he's missing the thumb on his left hand. I don't think the war's fully over for him yet, and I think the same goes for plenty of other people in this country too...

Mme Burlaud just suggested something crazy weird: a skiing trip organized by the city. She went on and on about how it'd be really good for me, how I'd meet some people, get away from the neighborhood. She said it might help me open up.

I don't want to go because I don't want to leave my mom on her own, even if it's just for a week. Anyway, a group vacation with people I don't get to choose, no way! Even just the ride...not in your dreams. Eight hours in a bus that reeks of puke, where everyone's singing songs from the eighties and we take piss stops every half hour? Forget it.

At first, Mme Burlaud thought I didn't want to go because of the cash.

"You know how it works. The trip's funded, we've already talked about it. It won't cost your mom anything, if that's what's worrying you…"

Whatever, skiing sucks. It's like sledding, except you're standing up wearing a silly hat and a big fluorescent fat suit. I know, I've seen ski competitions on TV.

I'm sure Mme Burlaud spends some time every winter at the ski resort, but she never actually does any skiing. She just lounges around on the patios with a hot chocolate, a pink pom-pom hat, and her husband nearby taking photos with a disposable camera. Come to think of it, does she even have a husband? Never thought about that. That's what's so tired about psychologists, psychiatrists, psychoanalysts, and all things that start with *psy*… They want you to tell them your life story, but them, they don't tell you one thing about themselves. Mme Burlaud knows stuff about me I don't know about myself. After you realize all that, you don't want to talk to them anymore. It's a rip-off.

Now, our social worker, though, she'll take any excuse to tell you her whole life story. I found out through Mom she was getting married. And so right off I'm thinking, why did she need to tell her that? We don't give a shit if she's getting married. Yeah, OK, so she's lucky. We get the picture, no need to make a big deal about it. Still, at least now she'll actually have a reason to be smiling all the time. So that'll get on my nerves a lot less.

Yeah, all right, so maybe I'm jealous. When I was little, I used to cut the hair off Barbie dolls because they were blond, and I chopped off their boobs too because I didn't have any. And they weren't even real Barbie dolls. They were like poor people's dolls, the kind my mom bought me at that cheapo discount store Giga. Crappy dolls. You played with them for two days and they looked like land-mine victims. Even their first name was total shit: Françoise. Not exactly the kind of name that little girls' dreams are made of! Françoise—that's the name of a doll for little girls who don't even dare to dream.

When I was younger, I dreamed of marrying a guy who'd make everybody else look like losers. Regular guys, the ones who put two months into making shelves from a kit or do a twenty-five-piece puzzle

with AGES 5 AND UP on the box, no thanks. I saw myself more with MacGyver. A guy who can unclog
your toilet with a can of Coke, fix the TV with a Bic
pen, and give your hair a perfect blowout with his
breath. A human Swiss Army knife.

I'm picturing a super wedding, an all-out reception
that would make people dizzy, a white dress with tons
of lace all over, a beautiful veil and a long train, at
least fifty feet. There'd be flowers and white candles.
My witness would have to be Hamoudi, and the
bridesmaids would be those three little sisters from
the Ivory Coast who're always playing jump rope in
front of our building.

Trouble is, the one who leads me down the aisle is
supposed to be my asshole of a father. But since he
won't even be there, we'll have to call the whole thing
off. The guests'll take back their wedding presents
and snag food from the buffet to take home with
them. Anyway, who gives a shit, before you start
thinking about a wedding it helps to find a husband.

Our generation's lucky because you get to choose
who you're going to love for the rest of your life. Or
the rest of the year. Depends on the couple. In *For-
bidden Zone,* Bernard de La Villardière was talking

about the divorce problem. He was explaining why it was on the rise. Only reason I can see for this is *The Young and the Restless.* In that TV series, they've all been married to each other at least once, if not twice. The story lines are totally crazy and my mom, she's been following every plot twist since 1989. All the neighborhood ladies are so into it. They meet up in the square to get the full lowdown on episodes they missed. They're way worse than that shameful boy band phase, when we were all fanatics. I remember a girlfriend giving me a poster of Filip from 2 Be 3 that she'd cut out of a magazine. Crazy happy, I stuck it on my bedroom wall. In this photo Filip was almost too much, with ultrawhite teeth that were practically see-through they were so clean, and he was shirtless with a bulging six-pack straight out of a cartoon. That evening my dad came into my bedroom. He lost it and started ripping down the poster, shouting: "I won't have any of this trash in my house, it's the devil's work, it's Satan!" It's not exactly how I'd pictured the devil, but there you go...On my empty wall there was just one tiny scrap of poster left with Filip's nipple on it.

on the school front, the trimester ended as badly as it started. It's a good thing my mom can't read. Well, you know, I mean as far as my report card goes... If there's one thing that bugs me, it's teachers who get all competitive about who writes the most original report-card comments. End result: They're all as screwed up and stupid as the others... The worst I ever saw was Nadine Benbarchiche, our physics and chemistry teacher, who wrote: "Exasperating, hopeless, the kind of student who makes you want to resign or commit suicide." She must have thought she was being funny or something. I'll give her that. It's true that I'm useless, but, really, there's no need to cross that line. Whatever, I don't give a shit. She wears thongs. So, anyway, the kind of comments I keep getting, the ones I call skip-repeat comments, are stuff like: "seems lost" or "seems somewhere else," or, worse, really pathetic lines like: "Get your head out of the clouds! Earth to Doria!" The only one who wrote anything nice about me was Madame Lemoine, the drawing teacher, oops, sorry, make that Plastic Arts. She put: "Malleable skills." Yeah, OK, it doesn't really mean anything, but it was nice of her anyway.

Even though I've got my malleable skills, a friend of Mom's suggested that her son help me with my homework. According to her I'll get better than As, because her son Nabil's a genius. I pointed out that Arab mothers usually think that way about their sons. But Nabil's mom, she's way over the top. She thinks he's the Einstein of the projects and she's always going on and on about him to everybody. And he plays into it, all just because he wears glasses and knows a little about politics. Sure, he's probably got a vague idea what the difference is between right and left. Luckily, my mom didn't exactly say yes. She played that wildcard, aka "inshallah." It doesn't mean yes or no. The real translation is "God willing." But, thing is, you can't ever know if God's willing or not...

Nabil's a nobody, a loser. He's got acne and when he was in elementary school, almost every day at recess he got bullied into handing over his snack. A big fat victim. Me, I prefer heroes, like in the movies, the kind of guy girls dream about...Al Pacino, I'll bet you nobody could take his snacks. Straight up, he'd pull out his semiautomatic and blow your thumb off, so you couldn't suck it at night before you fell asleep. All done.

So for the past few weeks, Nabil's been coming over to my place every so often to help me with my homework. This guy, he talks about himself way too much! Thinks he knows it all. Last time, he laughed in my face because I thought *Zadig* was a brand of car tire. Yeah, OK, so now I know it's this Babylonian satire by Voltaire. But he kept snickering for like forty-five minutes just because of that...At one point, he saw it didn't make me laugh one bit, and he said: "Aw, no worries, I'm only kidding. You know it's no big deal, in life there are intellectuals and there's everyone else." Fool. His mother just dumped him on me. Bet she just wanted to get rid of him...

But fine, I'll give Nabil credit for extenuating circumstances because it can't be easy dealing with his mom every day. She's always on his case. At first I thought Nabil's name was "Myzon" because that's what she kept calling him and all the time she'd be petting his head. Word is, she watches over him like her life depends on it, wants to know everything about his girlfriends, his private life, etc. Yeah, OK, so he hasn't got a private life, but, still, it's kind of unfair. Even when he was little, she'd show up at break to hand him sugar cookies through the school railings. Everyone in the neighborhood says at their house the mom is the dad, and the kids never stop giving him shit.

"Hey, Nabil! Your dad does the dishes, right! And your mom wears the boxers!"

See, I'm making like those attorneys in American films who defend a client who's a serial killer, rapist, and cannibal by telling you the whole horrible story of his terribly unhappy childhood. That way the jury feels sorry for him and they kind of forget the fact that sixteen-year-old Olivia's thigh is still in his freezer...

But the way I see it, Nabil should be even nicer to other people. Especially since his mom messed up his life big time and made him read Jesus's biography when he was eleven.

Me, I don't know if I'll want kids later. Anyway, I'd never make them read Jesus's bio, or say hello to old people if they didn't want to, or clean their plates...

And then again, maybe I've already had enough of kids, because in eighth grade our bio teacher showed us a birth, full-frontal, and it seriously turned me off to procreation.

I talked about it with Mme Burlaud last Monday, but that session she was kind of acting weird. She wasn't listening to me too well. I guess she looked preoccupied. I wonder if she sees a shrink. She should, it'd be good for her...

Lately, she's really losing it. She makes me play with Play-Doh. The shapes I make, they don't look like anything, but she smiles:

"Yes, OK, that's interesting!"

"That's interesting" doesn't mean anything. Something trashy can be interesting for its trashiness. This whole exercise is just for show, too. On the other hand, that's what I like about Mme Burlaud: She never judges. She always takes you seriously, even when you're making an apartment tower out of lilac Play-Doh.

Then we talked about something new that's happened to me. I've got my period. To tell the truth, I was kind of behind the other girls. The school nurse told me it was hereditary. Hereditary means it's your mom's fault. Mom got hers when she was about fifteen too. That must have been too cool for her because back in the *bled* they didn't even have sanitary pads. Before, I used to think periods were blue, like in the Always ad, the one where they talk about menstrual flow and liquids and stuff, the one that always comes on while we're eating dinner.

Mme Burlaud asked me tons of questions. It's like she's completely obsessed with periods. Has she ever had her own or what?

She told me lots of girls are freaked out the first time they start bleeding. And then she explained how periods are only the beginning, I'm going to get chest pains because of my breasts growing, and I'll definitely get zits on my face too. Nice. Why not greasy hair, a gawky body, and glassy eyes like every other teenager? I'd rather throw myself out the window of my low-income housing.

I've noticed people always make themselves feel better by looking at other people worse off than they are. So that evening I cheered myself up by thinking about poor Nabil.

εvεɾy yεαɾ people start preparing way in advance for the Livry-Gargan summer fair. Parents, kids, and especially the neighborhood gossips, because at the street fair, you can get your gossip fix for sure.

This year there were plenty of games for the kids, food stands with mint tea and sweet Middle Eastern pastries, Elie's barbecued *merguez* sausages and fries (Elie's like our neighborhood social planner), plus a stage with bands playing one right after the other. Local kids from the projects stepped up to rap. They even had some girls singing with them. Yeah, OK, so the girls just joined in for two pathetic chorus lines and the rest of the time, they were kind of stuck there making fools of themselves, just waddling around waving their hands in the air. But it wasn't so bad really. One more step toward equality...

Mom made me play the fishing game. I did it just to make her happy, but it was way out of hand. Average age of the other players: 7.3 years. And the only prize I could even catch was a one-eyed rag doll with freckles. I was too embarrassed.

Afterward, Mom and me headed over to see Cheb Momo. He's been singing at the Livry-Gargan summer fair every year since 1987, with the same musician, same synthesizer, and, of course, same songs. It's not too bad because everybody ends up knowing all the words by heart, even the people who don't speak a word of Arabic. Plus, what's good about Cheb Momo is that everything's real vintage, like his black jacket with gold sequins. He makes himself out like a real dreamboat and it works! Every year, it's the same ooh-la-la frenzy with all the neighborhood ladies.

I ran into Hamoudi at the fair. When I went over to say hey to him, I noticed he was with a girl. I smiled at her the way girls are supposed to, like I was actually happy to meet her, except I wasn't at all.

Hamoudi grinned at me with his slightly rotten teeth and said:

"Doria, uh…this is Karine…and, um…Karine, this is Doria…" He said it like an idiot, and like he was suddenly thirty years older. Plus, he was wearing a Hawaiian shirt that was way too ugly.

It felt like we were in a scene out of a Sunday night made-for-TV movie on that cable channel M6. I was all upset. So I looked at the girl and made like:

"See ya, Karim…"

I didn't even realize what I was saying. They stared at me all big-eyed and shocked. Both of them looked like Pokémon.

I went back to see Mom and, for the first time, we stayed through to the end of the festival. All the other years, Dad would always find us and take us back to the apartment. He never liked us just hanging around. I always had to watch the close of the fair from our living room window.

The Hamoudi story has got me sad. I'd been all worried because it had been a long time since I'd seen him. I'd even talked about it with Mme Burlaud. And then he goes and turns up at the fair with a girl named Karim on his arm, some trashy blond perched on fifteen-inch heels. When I went to bed, my head was full of all this sad music, like in those life insurance ads. And you know, Hamoudi had shaved so smooth, he smelled like lavender air freshener, and his eyes weren't even bloodshot. He didn't look like himself at all. This chick Karim's totally transformed him. Who knows, maybe she's worked black magic on him. I get a weird feeling about her. She even looks shady, if you ask me, with all that off-tone pancake foundation smeared on her face.

My mom's told me crazy scary stories about witch-craft back in Morocco. When she was young, one of her neighbors had a curse put on her at the souk, like a month before she was supposed to get married. Next thing you know, she goes bald and the wedding's canceled. Gotta watch your back. It can happen to anybody. Now that I think about it, we've all got someone who might want to do us wrong... Maybe Mme Burlaud's put a spell on her felt-tip pens and Play-Doh so I'll be in the same shit all my life, and that way I have to keep coming to see her Mondays at 4:30 until the day I die.

That reminds me of something. Last year I collected those marabout flyers that the Hindus hand you at the top of the exit escalator on the metro. Normal people collect stamps, postcards, or corks. I collect witch-doctor propaganda.

MONSIEUR KABA
International experience and reputation.
Thoughtful, efficient, fast, discreet.

He solves every kind of problem, strengthens and encourages feelings of affection, love, consideration, fidelity between spouses, social status, driver's licenses, luck, success…

Open every day from 8 A.M. to 9 P.M.

*Results are not guaranteed— first consultation: 35 euros

I figure if this actually worked, we'd all be happy, and people like Mme Burlaud or Mme DuGizmo, the social worker from city hall, they'd all be unemployed.

I bet Karim the Blond goes to see people like this guy Kaba. Hamoudi doesn't need a girl like her, because now he looks like those guys—their hair all straight, perfectly plastered with gel—who go door to door selling encyclopedias. I know Hamoudi. It's not like him to be all clean-cut.

When I went to bed, I took out one of the books I found in a box dumped outside our building. These were trashy books I'd never read normally. Romance-style Barbara Cartland-ish books but the worst kind, with a pitiful cover: a couple all sweetly interlocked, planted like two jerks against a dreamscape, just like in the catalog photos for Tati Vacations. If you want to read this kind of pulp on the metro, you'd best cover it with brown paper, or else fat-man Francis who's reading *Le Figaro*, all smug, his mouth pursed with this too-good-for-you pout, might just take the chance to call you out.

The book I picked up was called *Saharan Love at First Sight* and I have to admit I kept reading until I finished, late that night. The story's about this desert nomad called Steve—so already, this early on, you know it's total fiction—and Steve, he rescues a young red-haired teacher who's on vacation and gets all bloodied up in an accident with a camel. The guy is built like mule-head Rachid and his name is Steve, but this lady, that doesn't bother her one bit. So she falls in love with this guy she doesn't even know, someone she's just met between sand dunes. It's so ridiculous, you can't believe it for a second, and it's full of clichés, but even so, you fall for it full on. You even end up identifying with this total mental patient who's running a fever and keeps hallucinating, all because she fell off her camel.

resterday, when I went to pay the rent for Mom, the super's wife—the one who's still sporting the perm she got at the hairdresser's in 1974—told me about a new tenant in the neighborhood who's looking for someone to babysit her daughter. She said if I was interested, I should go see her and offer my services.

"Wouldn't you like to earn some cash?"

I thought it was nice of her to think of me; seriously, she could have suggested it to any of the girls in the neighborhood, but no, she thought of me. I take back everything I said about her, the perm and all the rest...

"That way, you'll be able to dress like the other kids your age, right?"

At the time, I didn't really know how to take that. It almost gave me a nosebleed. Even the fossil who works as the building custodian is mocking me. If I'd wanted to, I could have given that comment right back to her in the teeth. But, like a chump, I just said:

"Yeah, thank you, I'll go see her, bye!"

"Wait a minute, you're six centimes short, I can't stamp your rent book."

Stupid old cow. I just keep telling myself it would be too cool to make a little money. I'll never be six centimes short on the rent again.

Lila is the name of the woman who is looking for someone to watch her daughter. She's thirty. I don't know why, but I imagined her older. I figured she must work at a department store like Galeries Lafayette, and her freezer, it would be stocked full of frozen meals. Turns out she's a cashier at the Continent supermarket in Bondy and she knows how to cook. She wears this thin, even stripe of eyeliner on her eyelids, she has pretty brown hair that sticks up, a beautiful smile, and a southern accent because she grew up in Marseille. Oh, and she reads a whole mess of women's magazines with bullshit tests like: "Are You Possessive?" or "What Kind of Seductress Are You?"

We saw each other for less than half an hour. She asked me a few questions, then she said that in any case it was written all over my face that I was a good person. She introduced me to her daughter, Sarah. She's only four but she seems alert, intelligent, and very irresistible, while usually I think kids...

Lila separated from Sarah's dad just recently. So that's why she came to live in this development. She told me a little bit about what happened. Her eyes were all full of bitterness. He must have taken everything from her. Even her Daniel Guichard and Frank Michaël compilations that were in her dresser drawer.

"If I pay you three euros an hour, will that work?"

She just came out with it, without me expecting it or anything. Thing is, she was all worked up because she didn't think three euros was very much, but it was all she could do right now. She had no idea that for me, three euros an hour, it's a real fortune. So then I just said:

"Yeah, that works. Thank you."

gets her job

And it was a real thank you, the kind you say when you really mean it, when you're happy and you practically have tears stinging at the corners of your eyes.

I've got to pick up Sarah from the rec center at 5:30 and keep her at my house until Lila comes to take her home. I'm happy to do that. I would have liked to have talked it over with Hamoudi, but I don't see him anymore. He must be with that twit Karine playing Clue in her little made-in-Ikea living room.

When I told Mom I was going to do some baby-sitting, she wasn't happy. She told me that she was capable of taking care of us all by herself, that she could provide... She was on the verge of tears. At dinner, neither of us said a word. And it wasn't like it always seems in the movies, but like real life. And even if in the end she said it was OK, I knew she was still pissed.

Rɪɢʜᴛ ɴᴏᴡ at the Formula 1 Motel in Bagnolet, everything's gone to shit. Lots of Mom's coworkers are on strike. They've managed to work something out with the unions so their demands get heard.

The woman in charge of the strike at the Formula 1 is Fatouma Konaré, a coworker Mom gets along with well. She told me that at the beginning she thought *"Fatoumakonaré"* was just her first name and it seemed kind of long for a first name...Fatouma started working at the Bagnolet motel in 1991. Back then, I didn't even know how to tie my shoelaces by myself. It was Fatouma who started making noise about women workers being exploited at the motel.

Mom told me she'd like to go on strike with the other girls, but she can't. Fatouma and the others, they've got their husbands to help them, but us, we're all alone. Result: With most of the other maids on strike, Mom has a thousand times more work.

M. Winner, the dumbass who plays at being their boss, this must really piss him off. Serves him right. Mom told me he's already laid off some of the maids who are on strike, even though he's got no right. He fired this Vietnamese woman who works the same hours as Mom, for a false cause. It's really disgusting. He's going straight to hell and he's going to be hurting, he'll be making every kind of bodily gesture while shouting: "It's hot! It burns!" But who knows, in his private life M. Winner could be a nice guy who spends his time smiling, giving to charity, and chasing after people who park in handicapped spaces.

Maybe Mme Burlaud has it right when she says I can't stand it when someone passes judgment on me but that I do it all the time to other people. Except with M. Winner it's not so bad, because when I call him a bastard I have a minuscule margin of error.

———

There's a strike at school too. It's like everything around me has stopped. It's only been going on a few days but I feel like it's lasted forever. M. Loiseau, the principal, was mugged in the hall by a student from somewhere else. I wasn't there, but word is, this guy gassed M. Loiseau in the face with some teargas. That man has no luck at all. The one time he actually leaves his office to make sure the building is still standing, he gets gassed.

Ever since, it's total misery at school. Three quarters of the teachers no longer bother teaching class. Mme Benbarchiche's even been sticking up posters everywhere that say: NO MORE VIOLENCE! or some other pseudo-shock-value slogans, all worthy of a road-safety campaign. It's funny because since the start of the strike, she's been super active. It would be kind of nice if she put as much energy into her classes as she does into her posters. Could be that she's a secret militant. Hard core. A woman with a real political conscience. From time to time she might even send the occasional check to Chirac's UMP party, even if she doesn't look like she'd be the type, with her crow black dyed hair and her fuchsia lipstick.

———

The only one who isn't on strike is Monsieur Lefèvre, the one who talks like Pierre Bellemare, that presenter from the old home shopping channel. For him, this strike is all a sham, and the attack on M. Loiseau is just an easy excuse for all these deadbeat teachers to be even lazier.

Me, I think what's happened is serious. I'm not saying M. Loiseau is the nicest guy in the zip code, but, still, things shouldn't have gone down like that. And even before he was gassed, it's wrong that Loiseau only really felt safe in his office.

Whatever, not many students support the strike. It's like most of them think it won't make any difference and that we're hopelessly screwed anyhow...

LAST WEEK, Mme DuThingy, the social worker from city hall, came back to the house. This woman, she's really a shit-stirrer. Mom had hardly opened the door when she flashed her perfect white teeth and started up:

"Oh dear, you don't look so good...oooh la la."

Bet the reason she's all busting out is because she just finished that course of twelve free tanning sessions she got for being such a good customer at that health-and-beauty salon Pretty Kisser. Oh and then she went around our apartment at least ten times like she was visiting the catacombs or something.

"You really should think about changing the joint on the kitchen faucet."

She said it with that superior air she knows how to take on way too easily. I wonder if she didn't choose this career because it makes her feel better to busy herself with other people's misery. Mom went to all the effort of making mint tea for her, but she barely took a sip.

"It's really very good..." (She puckered her lips like she was sucking on a lemon.) "But it is...um... very sweet...I really have to pay attention to my figure...and you know what they say...once they're married, women tend to let themselves go..."

She started into a fit of giggling with her brittle, tinkling laugh, eyes closed and hand close to her mouth, Marilyn Monroe style. Who does she think she is? She needs to get over herself, she's only been married a month, this freak.

Mom, she didn't give a shit. She just giggled along with her. It seems to me that all this, it doesn't get to her one bit. I watched her talking, sitting with the next Miss France, and I thought that's how I'd like to be. Mme DuGizmo knocked Mom's appearance, her faucet, and her mint tea, and still she didn't give a damn. She just kept on giggling and talking with her.

She even told her about the strike and the situation over at the Formula 1. With that, Mme DuThingamjig put on this very grave face and suggested Mom sign up for a literacy course at this adult-learning center in Bondy. She'd learn how to read and write and at the same time she'd get help finding a new job. Mom wouldn't have to pay anything. The course is run by the Livry-Gargan city hall.

Before leaving, she looked at me while she was digging around in her "Looey Vweeton" bag, and then went:

"I've got something for you."

She said it in that high-pitched voice of hers, dragging out each syllable of the sentence, making her seem even more retarded. I felt eight months old and like she was announcing to me that she was going to change my diaper now or give me a little pot of artichokes to slurp.

Turns out, she gave me a reading coupon so I can get free books. I feel like I'm going backward with all these people treating me like a welfare junkie. Go to hell, all of you.

―――――

When she closed the door, I thought we were all done for the evening, but then the phone rang. It was Aunt Zohra in a panic because the police showed up at her place at six in the morning to arrest Youssef. They broke the door down, kicked him out of bed, turned the whole house upside down, and took him to the station. Aunt Zohra couldn't stop crying, not on the telephone at least. She told Mom that he's mixed up in drug dealing and some business with stolen cars. I'm pretty sure she thought it was her fault because she hadn't been taking close enough care of her son. By the end of the conversation, Mom couldn't stop crying either.

I guess right now Youssef's being interrogated in a stuffy gray office. Me, I know that Youssef's one of the good guys. It's not fair. When Mom hung up, we talked a bit but there are times when even words aren't enough. So we just stared out the window and that said it all. Outside, it was gray like the color of our building's concrete and it was drizzling in very fine drops, as if God were spitting on all of us.

ғor the past several nights I've had the same dream, one of those crazy heavy dreams you remember perfectly when you wake up and that you can describe to someone down to the last detail.

I was opening the window and I had the sun coming down on my face full force. I couldn't even get my eyes open. I put my legs through the window just until I was sitting on the edge, then, with one strong push, I took flight. I kept going higher and higher, I saw the apartment towers getting farther away and growing smaller and smaller. I flapped my wings, uh, make that my arms, and then, because I was trying so hard to keep gaining height, I went truly smack-bash into this wall on my right and it gave me a massive bruise. That's what woke me up and I have to say it was kind of hard coming back to reality like that.

I told Mme Burlaud my dream. She kept looking at me, blinking her eyes, and said:

"Yes, of course, absolutely... It's like the episode with the atlas..."

Right. She calls it an episode, straight out. For all I know, Mme Burlaud isn't really a shrink. Maybe she works in TV and all the bullshit I tell her feeds into her sitcom. Burlaud, I bet that's a pseudonym, and her real name's something in the style of Laurence Bouchard. She's part of the scriptwriting team working for AB Productions. That's got to be it... Maybe the concept is already being made into a series, it will be a smash hit and get broadcast all over the world. It will even be dubbed into Japanese. And me? I don't hold any rights. I'll just be one of the millions of fans, faceless and fucked over, like all the rest.

The Atlas Episode, I don't even know why I told her about that. I don't know why I tell her any of the other stuff either... This was a day when I was bored out of my mind. I went to the junk room to find the atlas I got as a prize at the end of fifth grade.

A junk room's like an attic, but a little smaller, generally in the hallway. It's for all the crap you never need.

Basically, I opened my atlas at the planisphere, that place where the whole world fits on a single page. I was having sort of a rough time, so I drew an escape route on the map. It was the route I was going to take one day, going through all of the most beautiful places in the world. Yeah, OK, so I drew the route in pencil because Mom would have let loose on me if she'd seen me scribbling in pen all over a new book. But, anyway, I did draw this perfect route once, even if I'm still at the departure point and the departure point is Livry-Gargan.

Anyhow, I don't know if Mom would be OK with me splitting like that. There wouldn't be anyone around to record *The Young and the Restless* for her. And nobody to go and pick up Sarah from the center. And Lila, she'd be screwed having to find another babysitter. It reminds me that there are some people who need me, after all, and that makes me feel sort of good.

Because, sometimes, I just really would like to be
someone else, somewhere else, and maybe in a whole
different time. Often, I imagine I'm part of the Ingalls family from *The Little House on the Prairie.*

Here's the way it works:

Dad, Mom, kids, dog that doesn't bite, barn, and
ribbons in your hair for going to church on Sunday
mornings. You know, happiness...The story, it all
takes place in this pre-1900 period atmosphere, with
oil lamps, the arrival of the railroad, prehistoric
clothes, and other old stuff like that...The thing I
like about the Ingalls family is that as soon as some
big drama starts up, they make the sign of the cross,
have a good little crying session, and by the next
episode everybody's forgotten all about it...It's pure
movie magic.

It's too embarrassing because I think the characters
in that series are better dressed than me. Even though
they live in this shitty microvillage and their dad's
some fat farmer. Take the hoodie I'm wearing right
now, not even the Salvation Army would want it.
Once, I was wearing this lavender sweatshirt with
stars and something written in English on it. My mom,
she bought it in a secondhand store that smelled like

lots of old musty stuff. She paid only one euro for it. She was all proud. I didn't want to upset her, so I wore it to school but, I don't know, I had a bad feeling about it, the sweatshirt seemed shady. It was. The fat bitches at school, that crew of bad dye-jobs, all made up with their padded bras and stacked heels, they never let me hear the end of it. The thing written in English on the sweatshirt, it meant "sweet dreams." That piece-of-shit lavender sweatshirt was actually a pajama top. I knew that I should have paid more attention in Miss Baker's fifth-grade English lessons.

coming out of school, I ran into Hamoudi.
He offered me a ride, said he'd drop me off in our
neighborhood. I was so proud I kind of flaunted it, so
all those jerks could see me leaving with Antonio
Banderas's double from *Zorro*, except a bit more
scarred. But nobody saw it. No big deal.

All things considered, it suits him wearing cologne
and being clean-shaven. You get to see the scar on his
chin better. Gives him that tormented-soul look, rebel
with a heart of gold, that kind of thing...Like the heroes in the movies. The day I asked him how he got
it, he said he couldn't remember. Basically, he didn't

want to tell me. Hamoudi can be so annoying sometimes, when he plays Mr. Mystery Man.

I noticed it wasn't the same car he had last week.
Hamoudi's always changing cars. Either he's got a
car-dealer buddy who's in love with him, or he's
working some shady stuff, in which case I can't
ask him any questions. That's how it is, between
Hamoudi and me. He wants to protect me, doesn't
want me mixed up in his affairs, so the deal is I curb
my curiosity.

When I got into the car, I just said hello without
even looking at him, even though I could see he was
staring at me. He didn't start the engine and I could
feel him still looking at me. It was stressing me out.

After a while, he turned my face toward him,
smiled at me, and said:

"Don't worry! You'll always be my favorite!"

And then he started giggling. Even though part
of me wanted to keep being mad, I started laughing
with him, because what he said, it took a load off me.
Hamoudi was talking about that Karine girl I saw
him with at the street party, with her Frisbee face and
high heels. Maybe he thought I was jealous or something…Whatever. Anyway, she doesn't go with any-

thing about him, she's blond and wears mauve. See that relationship working? Me neither.

Actually, it's good for him he's met this girl. At the least, something's going on in his life. With me, it's just *kif-kif* tomorrow. Same shit, different day.

When Hamoudi dropped me off at our building, Aziz, the neighborhood grocer, was waving at me big time. Seeing him reminded me that maybe we need someone else at home. A man who wouldn't run off to the other side of the Mediterranean or split with a peroxide blond in high heels. But except for Aziz, who seems a little bit in love with Mom, I don't really see who it could be…

Aziz, he's gotta be around fifty. He's short, practically bald, always has dirty nails, and spends his time trying to dislodge stuff from his teeth with the tip of his tongue. At the Sidi Mohamed Market, there's a lot of stuff past its expiration date and he makes you pay more if you take a soda from the little fridge at the back instead of the front counter. He even used to sell bread, until one day a customer found a cockroach in a baguette and called the health inspector. On Eid, Aziz gives Mom a bag full of groceries, and when we need it, he gives us credit, which we can't always repay. Sometimes he grumbles on in his villager accent: "Ooh la la! If you iz tiking creedeet after creedeet, you will never geet out to the othur side of the river!" He's a riot, Aziz. Whenever you go to pay, he always has a joke to tell you.

"Ze teacher ask Toto: 'At two euro a bottle how much is twelve bottles of wine?' And ze little boy he say what? He say: 'Three days, Miss...'"

And every time, he practically pisses himself from laughing so much. Even if he's a first-rate hustler, Aziz is nice. I bet lots of people like him around here. At least if Mom married him, we'd never need anything again. Yeah, OK, so he's not the boss of some swanky department store chain like Tati, but you never know, a few years from now there might be Sidi Mohamed Markets in New York and Moscow...

Mom's finally split from that skank stinky motel where she flushed the toilet after rich folks, all to be paid three times zero. M. Winner didn't even give her the back pay she was owed, made out like it was because of the strike, and all that... It's illegal, I just know it. Anyway, without Mom, M. Winner's motel's heading straight for bankruptcy. She's really got a way with making beds, kind of gentle but strong at the same time, in the end there isn't a single wrinkle on the sheet, better than the army. Me, personally, I'm very happy she's not working at the Formula 1 in Bagnolet anymore. Nothing there to miss. Not the hours, not the pay, and not that rat-head of a boss, M. Winner.

———

It's actually thanks to city social services. I say "actually" because it's not easy to admit that this Mme
DuDoohickey, the Barbie-doll social worker, helped
Mom find her alternating training. Alternating, that
means you're juggling two different things. Like when
you mix sweet and savory or husband and lover.
Mom, she's going to do a literacy course. They're
going to teach her to read and write in the language
of my country, this country. With a teacher, a black-
board, notebooks with big lines, and even homework.
I'm going to help her with it if she wants.

Me, I'm thinking lousy Nabil comes in handy when
I'm totally lost in chemistry and he explains the exer-
cises Mme Benbarchiche gives us to do. This time it's
the isotopes. But with her Tunisian accent, it comes
out sounding like "eezeetopes," almost like that rock
group of old bearded guys with their sunglasses...

It's funny because Mom's totally dreading this
course. She never went to school, so she's flipping.
Getting up at five o'clock in the morning to work in
some cheapskate motel and wreck her health, sure,
she doesn't give a shit. But now this, for her, it's no
joke. In this training they also teach about job-search

methods. With that, I'm hoping she'll find some supercool gig. She'll get paid while she's in training and she won't finish late at night, she's done at practically the same time as me. So now, I'll see her a lot more and it'll make it harder for me to forget so often that I even have a mother at all.

She's starting in just two weeks and it's freaking cool because in the meantime, at noon when I come home from school, I get to eat something other than canned tuna.

The thing Mom really likes watching on TV in the evenings is the weather. Especially when it's that newscaster with brown hair, the one who tried out for *La Cage aux Folles* but wasn't cast because he went too over the top... So there he was, talking about this huge cyclone in the Caribbean, this crazy thing getting ready to do serious damage. This hurricane, they called it Franky. Mom said she thinks this Western obsession with giving names to natural disasters is totally stupid. I like the times when Mom and me get a chance to have deep and interesting discussions.

AZIZ IS NICE AND ALL, but in his store you've got a one-in-three chance of getting spoiled goods, so sometimes I go to Malistar, a tiny minimarket that's been around for ages even if it's changed its name tons of times. At least ten different incarnations since I've lived here: World Provisions, Better Price, Touti-pri... It's confusing, because everyone calls this place something different, depending on which name stuck with them.

So I went to Malistar to buy some maxi pads, the generic kind, with the fluorescent orange package like the crossing-guard vests of those ladies who help kids

get to school first thing in the morning. Even just the
packaging is too much to bear. You really can't be
sly, and afterward everyone in the neighborhood
knows you've got your period. From the second I get
to the checkout, just my luck, the line's as long as the
Paris-Dakar race. And more like if the race went by
bike because it really wasn't moving very quickly...
When my turn finally came, another stroke of luck:
The packet wasn't scanning. It made this noise like a
scratched 45 each time the cashier tried swiping it.
The cashier, Monique, you could say she's got on her
game face. She's so flat you could fax her, and if I was
her, I'd have filed a suit against the hairdresser who
dared to give her that cut. Monique's got this great
sense of humor, which has to be from those Pierre
Palmade videos she watches on Sunday afternoons.
So, anyway, this damn pack of pads, Monique still
couldn't scan it and she'd had enough, but instead of
typing in the bar code like they do at the ATAC supermarket, she grabbed the microphone to make an an-
nouncement. Right there, my legs started shaking and
beads of sweat went sliding down my forehead like I
was one of those bomb-disarming experts about to

cut the red wire. She yells in that deep voice of hers—
she hadn't figured out there was no point shouting
since that's what mics are for:

"RAYMOND!!! How much is the twenty-four-
plus-get-two-free pack of sanitary napkins, regular
with absorbent padding and wings?!"

She waits a second and starts up again:

"Hello! Raymond! You asleep or what?"

Then we heard this voice from hell roaring that the
damn package was 2.38. The worst part, it's that I
didn't even have enough to pay for it and she had to
put it on credit. If I'd known, I definitely wouldn't
have had my period...

When I got back home, Mom was on the phone
again with Aunt Zohra. Youssef's case is coming to
court soon, so she's worried. Aunt Zohra calls Mom a
lot, even late at night, because she's having trouble
sleeping. They have these long conversations full of
silences. I know, because Mom uses speakerphone.

"I swear. Yasmina, my sister, you're lucky you never
had a son, God is with you, you have no idea..."

"...."

"I mean, with a daughter, it's easier! You know, I'd
never seen my son cry... Yesterday when I went to

visit him, he wept in my arms, like a woman. It breaks my heart you know..."

"May God come to your aid!"

"I hope he hears you, my sister... What am I going to say to the old man when he gets back from the *bled*? He'll be back in two months..."

"Beg God that your son comes home quickly..."

You could say the two of them are counting a lot on God. I hope Youssef will be free quickly. He doesn't deserve all this crap that's happening to him. Me, I don't know a thing about the law, the only references I have in this field are old episodes of *Perry Mason,* big-time lawyer. I even remember that there was one judge who fell asleep during the trial and people still called him "Your Honor."

If Youssef goes to prison, I understand nothing about justice.

ʜᴇ's ɡᴇᴛᴛɪɴɢ sᴇɴᴛ ᴜᴘ. They gave him a year. Aunt Zohra's disgusted with life. She's mostly scared of her crazy old husband, who gets back next month. Réda and Hamza, her two other sons, are in a free-fall at school and they're always busting up with other guys their age from the neighborhood because they keep getting called bastards seeing as their dad's practically never there. For Youssef, it's the big house, and even if he was always making fun of me, he really didn't deserve to lose a year of his life in such a stupid way.

It's like Hamoudi. After prison, he temped and did lots of shit odd jobs, each of them as much of a grind as the rest. He's never really managed to get it together since. These days, he lives off dealing and can't lead a normal life. Pensions and social security don't exist for dealers yet. But, in any case, I'd never have imagined this could happen to Youssef. If a clairvoyant told me about it a few months back, I wouldn't have believed her.

My mom told me that back in her country, when she was still at her parents' house, her aunt and their neighbor took her to see a clairvoyant. Everyone was all worried because Mom refused to get married. The clairvoyant told her that the man she was destined to marry would come from the other side of the sea to find her and that this man worked with earth and stone. In the end, it was my dad. It's true: He came to find her from the other side of the sea, from France; and by boat because it was cheaper than the plane. It's also true that he worked with earth and stone because, back then, he was in public buildings and works. But the clairvoyant, she kind of forgot to mention how it was going to end. People like that only say what you want to hear.

Take Shérif. Shérif, this guy from the neighborhood, he turned up from Tunisia about six years ago.
Everyone calls him Shérif because he's got a real
cowboy look going on. Plus, he always wears a red
cap with a star printed on it. He looks like he came
straight out of a Western, with his black hair and
mustache. So this guy went to see a clairvoyant who
told him that soon he'd be very rich. It's been years
since she told him that. Maybe she should have been
more specific about what she meant by "soon." So basically, ever since then, Shérif puts money on a trifecta for the horses every day, and he'd bet his life on
it making him rich. He goes to the bar in the square
to get the results. And since he loses every time, he
gets jittery. Shérif, he's a Mediterranean guy, right...
So when he doesn't win, which is every time, he
crumples his cap, shouts all these curses in Arabic,
and storms off. It's been like that a long time.

Sometimes I tell myself life's kind of lucky all the
same. We think we don't have much, but we don't
think about those people who have even less... Yeah,
yeah, they do exist. Like that boy at my primary
school who always got beaten up. Small blond kid
with glasses, had a season ticket for the front row in

class, always got the top grades, used to give the teacher pancakes on Shrove Tuesday, and ate pork in the school canteen. Your ideal victim.

Mom's started her new training. She likes it a lot, from what she tells me. She's even made friends with two other women: a Moroccan from Tangier and a Norman grandmother Mom calls "Jéquiline." I guess Jacqueline's the teacher. It reminds me that my mom's social, unlike me. When I was little and Mom took me to the sandbox, none of the other kids wanted to play with me. I called it the "French kids' sandbox," because it was right in the middle of a development with houses instead of towers and there were mostly full-blooded native French families living there. Once, they were all making a circle and no one would hold my hand because it was the day after Eid, the festival of the sheep, and Mom had put some henna on the palm of my right hand. Those morons thought I was dirty.

They didn't understand the first thing about social diversity and cultural melting pots. Then again, it wasn't really their fault. There's still such a well-drawn

line between the Paradise Estate where I live and the
Rousseau housing development. Massive wire fencing
that stinks of rust it's so old and a stone wall that runs
the whole length of the divide. Worse than the Mag-
inot Line or the Berlin Wall. On the project side, the
divider is covered in tags, drawings and concert posters
and flyers for different eastern-themed evenings, graf-
fiti praising Saddam Hussein or Che Guevara, patriotic
signs, VIVA TUNISIA, SENEGAL REPRESENT, even rap
lyrics with a philosophical slant. But me, what I like
best on the wall is an old drawing that's been there for
a really long time, long before the rise of rap or the
start of the war in Iraq. It's an angel in handcuffs with
a red cross over its mouth.

Samra experiences abuse

in my building, there's a girl being held prisoner on the tenth floor. Her name is Samra and she's nineteen. Her brother follows her everywhere. He stops her from going out and when she gets back from school a bit later than normal, he grabs her by the hair, then the dad finishes the job. Once, I even heard Samra screaming because they'd locked her in the apartment. In their family, the men are kings. They do serious close surveillance on Samra, and her mom can't say anything, can't do anything. So it's truly bad luck to be a girl.

Except a few days ago, some neighbors told Mom

Samra escaped. For the last three weeks everyone's been looking for her. Her dad even put in a police report. They stuck up posters all over, in shops, post offices, building lobbies, schools... The photo's from when Samra was in fifth grade. Her braces, they don't photocopy so well.

This makes me think of that TV show with Jacques Pradel where they would find people: *Lost from Sight*. There were even guys who hadn't seen members of their family for over twenty years. This show was too much. They managed to find people even if they'd changed their faces, names, and everything. Apart from when they were dead, it went like clockwork every time. Afterward, when they did the reunion bit, people were blubbering and fainting. It made the show feel kind of like a big spectacle. One time, they dug up this cousin in Sydney, Australia. They filmed his place, his new family, new job, and all that. I thought it wasn't so cool to show the guy who'd been cut up about the disappearance all those years, who had busted his ass to find his cousin only to realize the guy never gave a shit and had a great new life without him.

So, anyway, right now in the neighborhood, nobody talks about anything except Samra's disappearance. They're even saying people have seen her in Paris with a belly bump. Like she's already pregnant... The rumor goes from the grocery store to the school gates via the dry cleaner. When Samra was locked up at home in her concrete cage, nobody talked about it, like they found it completely normal. And now that she's managed to free herself from that dictator of a brother and torturer of a father, people are condemning her. I don't get it.

Now Youssef, he can't escape. Aunt Zohra called us again to tell us about her last visit. She never stops saying how he's getting skinny and his eyes are empty. She doesn't recognize her son anymore and I think it really scares her. Still, it seems to me like she's getting braver. She's putting on a better face about this whole ordeal than she did at the beginning. It took her a little time to get used to it, that's all. It's horrible to think how, if forced to submit, you can get used to anything, even the worst of it.

In two weeks Youssef's dad's coming back and I'm really wondering how that's going to go. Mom's helping Aunt Zohra come up with a plan. She says it's all about the way you announce these things. For bad news, you've got to get your inspiration from TV. Like Gaby's courage and tact on *Sunset Beach* when she tells her jerk of a husband that she cheated on him with his own brother. Oh yeah, and the brother was a priest. Even worse. So next to that, telling Youssef's dad his kid's in prison until next spring, it's a piece of cake. Like when I'm going to tell Mom I've got to repeat my classes from this year. First I'll have to explain what repeating means, because she hasn't got a clue when it comes to the school system. And then I'll tell her it's so I'm more successful. For her, success means working in an office with a chair that swivels and rolls, a telephone, and a radiator not too far from the chair that swivels and rolls.

The other evening, I hung around on the landing a little while shooting the shit with Hamoudi. We were talking about parents and the adolescent crisis because Mme Burlaud had explained to me what that meant.

Hamoudi thinks it's just an excuse, made up by Western parents who messed up raising their kids. I don't agree. Sometimes Hamoudi really goes to the extreme. He told me he wouldn't even have begun to think about having a tenth of an adolescent crisis because his dad would have known right away how to calm him down. He also told me it's over with Karine, that dumb blond I saw at the summer fair. When he said that, there was a little sadness in his voice. I know it's not right, but, deep down, it gave me a little pleasure. I was thinking how with Hamoudi and me, it was going to be the same as before. To cheer him up, I told him that, anyway, she had a face like a Frisbee. That cracked him up. Didn't tell me why they split up, though. I don't think she cheated on him with Hamoudi's brother who's not a priest.

He didn't tell me because he thinks these stories are for adults and none of my business. That's not completely wrong.

тhe other evening, that fat loser Nabil came over to help me with my civics homework. The subject sounded like one of those special reports on TV: "Why Don't People Vote?"

Lame-o Nabil and I really talked about it. For example, he says that a guy from the Paradise projects who left school a long time ago, who can't find a job, whose parents don't work, and who shares a bedroom with his four younger brothers: "Why would he give a shit about voting?" Nabil's right. The guy already has to fight daily just to survive, so you can forget about his duties as a citizen...If his situation improved a little, maybe he would want to get out and

vote. Still, I can't really see who'd make him feel rep-
resented. So there you go: This guy's the one to ask:
"Why Don't People Vote?" Not a class of zit-faced
fifteen-year-olds.

I wonder if this is why these housing develop-
ments are left to decay, because so few people around
here vote. You have no political usefulness if you
don't vote. Me, when I'm eighteen, I'll go vote. Here,
a person never gets a chance to be heard. So when we
get the chance, we have to take it.

Anyway, that evening, instead of leaving as soon
as we'd finished and going back to his mom's house,
Nabil just sat there, talking, finishing off the package
of crackers on the table. I thought those crackers
would last the week, but fine, too bad…When this
lameass finally decided to take off, I walked him
out, and right at the door his expression suddenly
completely changed. His face got all serious, he came
right up toward me, and he kissed me right on the
mouth. For real.

Not only does he stuff his face with all my crackers
but then he dares to kiss me without asking my opinion! The worst is that, like a dumb animal, I couldn't
think of anything to say. I just got all red like the

peppers my mom uses for sauce and blurted a barely audible "see ya" while I shut the door. After that, I ran and drank a giant glass of mint soda and brushed my teeth twice to get rid of the taste of Nabil.

What am I going to do now? I could try to make everyone believe that after falling off my bike, I lost consciousness and woke up with amnesia, that I don't remember anything else, really not one thing at all... The problem is that the story isn't credible. Everyone knows I don't have a bike or the money to buy one. Or wait, maybe I could get plastic surgery and become someone else so he doesn't recognize me and never tries gluing his fat chapped lips against mine again. Yuck.

It wasn't anything like how I'd imagined my first kiss. No, I saw it more in a dream setting, at the edge of a lake, in a forest, at sunset with a super guy who would look a little like the dude in the vitamin ads, the one who makes a little half turn in his chair, faces the camera dead-on with his toothpaste-white smile, and says: "If you're feeling well, it's Vitawell." My guy, he'd be in the middle of explaining how to start a fire with a nail file and a stone when, in the midst of our philosophical discussion, we'd start toward each other,

all gentle-like, and we'd kiss, like it was the most natural thing in the world, like we'd been doing it since
forever. Of course, when I imagine this scene, I've
got a real hairdo, I'm all stylish, and my chest is a little
bigger.

No one is in the know on the sad story of Nabil's
mouth. It's too nasty. Not even Mme Burlaud knows
and especially not Mom. If she finds out, she'll kill
me. I've got a grudge against Nabil for stealing my
first kiss and downing my package of saltines, but not
as much of one as I'd thought I would have. Well, I
know what I mean.

мondαy, at Mme Burlaud's, we did something new, like a game. She was showing me these large-format photos, flipping through them pretty fast, and I had to say "like it" or "don't like it."

Most of the time, since it was going so fast, I answered automatically without really having time to think. So for example, I found myself saying "don't like it" to the photo of a little baby. Mme Burlaud, playing like it was by accident, stopped on that photo. Like I hadn't seen it coming, she started talking about my so-called little half brother. Subconsciously, that's why I said: "Don't like it." Now, Mom and me, we know for sure it's a boy. A neighbor from Morocco sent us a letter. To make it even more humiliating, the letter was in French. I had to read it to her.

But seriously, why make something out of nothing? I told Mme Burlaud that the baby had nothing to do with it, that she was just going too fast and I didn't see the photo very well. I made a mistake, that's all... Well, shit. Nobody's obligated to like babies. Babies cry all the time, they stink and dribble and poop in their diapers... Plus, the baby in the photo was nasty ugly, like a fat croissant.

And, also, that brat isn't my brother. He's just the son of my father the Beard. It's not the same. Frankly, Mme Burlaud's tripping when she makes out like she's got an answer for everything and pastes that smug grin on her face like Harrison Ford at the end of every Indiana Jones movie. Right now, she's always telling me that I'm growing up and it's normal to have questions. I'm growing up... Shit, it's time she changed her glasses! I've been five foot two and three quarters a while now, and nothing's changing. Or maybe she meant growing up in my head. It must've been that...

———

To check Sarah's growth, Lila makes black pencil marks on the bedroom door and writes the dates next to them. It's funny, the door's covered in these little lines, one right on top of the other. When Sarah gets a little older, she'll get a kick out of seeing it again. And over at Sarah's there are photos everywhere of her from when she was tiny right up to now.

She's lucky. I don't have a single photo of me before I was three. After that, there are school photos...It makes me sad to think about, feels kind of like I don't completely exist. Bet if I'd had a dick, I'd have a big fat pile of photo albums, filled with pictures of me.

One day, coming back from the rec center with Sarah, we stopped to say hey to Hamoudi.

"So, princess, you're Sarah?"

"Yes."

"You're really cute in your pink dress, like a fairy..."

"Well you, your teeth aren't so nice, you should ask the tooth fairy to come visit you..."

I kind of let Sarah have it. I told her it wasn't nice

to talk like that. But Hamoudi couldn't have cared less. In fact, it made him die laughing. Fine, it's no lie Hamoudi's teeth are kind of busted. But they're not a complete disaster. Anyway, you'd expect it with everything he's smoked over the years...

So, anyway, that scene didn't stop him from being crazy about Sarah. He told me there's nothing more fresh than a kid, because they're sincere, spontaneous, genuine, you know... "They're the most honest thing in our hypocritical and corrupt society." Maybe Hamoudi's right... He's been really serious these days. Also, he's been looking hard for a job. Or that's what he told me. He has to go straight for a while because dealing is getting dangerous. And like he says, "I'm not seventeen anymore..." When he said that, he had regret in his eyes. "I'm nearly a third of the way through my life, and I've done nothing. Nada..." I told him it wasn't too late and if he was talking like that, maybe it was because he was scared of changing things. Don't know where I got that from. It has to be from watching daytime talk shows with themes like: "He cheated on me and yes it's my business." Still, it's strange Hamoudi's thinking that way because there's always been a fair amount of freedom in his family, he could do whatever he wanted. There was only one thing he couldn't do: cry. Because he's a man and Hamoudi's dad says men don't cry. Maybe that's what did it. People don't realize how important it is to cry.

IT'S ALREADY SUMMER VACATION. This afternoon I saw the Alis leave for Morocco. They've got this big red van and every year they cross France and Spain to get back to the *bled* and spend two months there. I was watching them from my window. They took at least an hour to load up. The kids were all dressed sharp. You could see from their faces how happy and excited they were to be leaving. I envied them. They were taking tons of luggage. Three quarters of those bags must have been full of presents for family, friends, and neighbors. It's always like that. The Mom Ali was even taking a vacuum cleaner. Rowenta's latest model. She'll get major respect over there with that thing.

———

Plus, they're going to see their place all finished. If you ask me, the fact that they built a house back in the *bled* by surviving on rice and pasta every meal so they could send every penny to the builders, and now the mom's taking a vacuum cleaner, it means they're planning on staying there. Bet it didn't even cross the kids' minds. But the parents, they must have been thinking about it ever since the first day they arrived in France. Ever since the day they made the mistake of setting foot in this crappy country they thought would become theirs.

Some people spend their whole lives hoping they'll make it back home. But a lot of them only go back once, in a coffin, shipped by plane like they're an export product or something. Apparently, they find home soil again, but it's definitely not the way they were expecting...

Then again, there are some who do manage to get back. Like the one who used to act the part of my dad. Except he left without his luggage.

Sometimes I try to imagine how I'd be if I were Polish or Russian instead of Moroccan...Maybe I'd do ice dancing, but not in those cheapskate local competitions where you win chocolate medals and T-shirts. No, real ice skating, like in the Olympics, with the most beautiful classical music, guys from all over the world who judge your performance like they do at school, and whole stadiums to cheer even if you go splat like a steak. Anyway, the most important thing is to do it with style. It's true that skating is the coolest: dresses covered in sequins, lots of organdy and colors...The trouble is that because of the outfits, you can always see the girls' underwear. So my mom, it wouldn't make her all that happy that I was ice dancing on TV. And another thing, if I were Russian I'd have a name that was all complicated to pronounce and I'd definitely be blond. I know, they're shitty prejudices. There must be Russian brunettes out there with names that are super simple to pronounce, so simple you'd shout them out for no other reason than the fun of saying such an easy name. I guess there even could be some Russian girls who have never laced up a pair of skates in their life.

So, meanwhile, everybody's taking off and I'm staying in the neighborhood to watch the projects like a guard dog waiting for everyone else to come back from vacation all tan. Even Nabil's disappeared. Maybe he left too, gone to Tunisia with his parents.

Anyway, since school's over, he won't be coming over to help me do my homework or write my papers. Actually, I'm done with papers for the rest of my life, except for on things like blowouts and curlers. Oh yeah, I didn't tell you: At school, they can't let me repeat the year because there aren't enough spots for everybody. And that "everybody" includes me. So they found me a place at the last minute at this technical school not so far from home, where I'll go for a hairdressing certificate. Hamoudi was crazy pissed off when I told him. He told me he was going to pay them a visit and complain, contact the school board, go off on the administration, and other stuff like that...He said they don't have the right to decide for me. I told him I didn't know what to do anyway, seeing as nobody's ever given me any career counseling. And plus, who knows, I might love hairdressing...It's true, giving perms to very old ladies who have three hairs on their skull and who pay a fortune to keep up their hair, I'm gonna like it, I can feel it...

There's a girl in the neighborhood who did hairdressing school. She doesn't have enough money to
open her own salon but she still wants to be her own
boss, so she does hair at home. It works pretty well.
When there's a wedding in the neighborhood, everyone calls her. The girls get blowouts, have major work
done on their hair, where it's pulled and yanked extra
tight so it looks naturally straight. But at the party,
after one or two dances, they start sweating and a few
curly wisps start to give them away...

Speaking of weddings, there's one happening
soon. It's Aziz, our famous businessman from the
Sidi Mohamed Market, the stingiest grocer on earth.
I'm a little sick he's getting married, because that
means it's over for Mom...

Rachida, our neighbor who's also the worst gossip
I know, told us Aziz is going to marry a girl from
Morocco. I'm starting to see why there're so many
single women here. If all these men are getting into
import-export... It's a shame our weddings aren't like
in the States where the priest says that famous line:
"If anyone here objects to this union, let them speak
now or forever hold their peace." And, there's always
some supercourageous guy who dares to interrupt

the ceremony because he's been secretly in love with the bride for eight years. So he tells her, and with tears in her eyes, she says she feels the same way. The husband's a good loser—even if he's kind of pissed— and shakes the hand of the supercourageous guy and says: "No hard feelings, old pal!" Then he lends him the tux he rented for a fortune just for the occasion and the gutsy guy marries the girl in place of the good-loser-groom.

Mom could do the same thing at Aziz's wedding. She could tell Aziz he's the most romantic guy in the neighborhood and she's had strong feelings for him for years despite his bald head and his grubby nails. I have got to stop thinking in movies. I know she'd never do that. Plus, the whole neighborhood's going to be at Aziz's wedding and if Mom did that, it'd be too shameful. We call it *hchouma*. Anyway, it's not even for sure that he's inviting us. He's given us so much credit we've never paid back. And no one ever invites us anywhere. Ages after a party people come to see Mom to say they're sorry they forgot about her. No big deal. Mom and me don't give a shit about being part of the jet set.

sunday morning, Mom and me, we went to a rummage sale. She was hoping to find some shoes because in her left shoe there's a small hole up by her toe and when it rains or she walks on the grass in the morning her toes get soaked.

We were walking in the aisles between the stands when I heard these girls behind us:

"Check out that girl, dressed even worse than her old lady...It's like when they were rummaging for stuff to sell they found her too!"

"Yeah, right. For them a rummage sale is like the Galeries Lafayette..."

They lost it laughing. Little mean snickers, all stifled and shit. I looked at Mom. Apparently, she didn't hear a thing. She was concentrating on this old 45 sleeve of Michel Sardou. In the photo, he still had this big head of shag hair. It's like they repatriated all the hairdressers in the eighties, hid them in a cave, and then they only started reappearing at the beginning of the nineties.

So those two bitches who said that right behind our backs, I didn't even turn around to eat them alive or cut their nostrils into teeny bits. No, I made like nothing had happened, like I hadn't heard. I took Mom by the arm. I squeezed it because I was still feeling full of hate and then I felt tears welling up in my eyes and my nose was stinging. I really wanted to cry, but I was trying to keep my cool. I forced myself, because I didn't want to tell Mom the whole story. She'd have felt like it was her fault. And, anyway, she was checking out these bunches of vegetable peelers for one euro, so I didn't want to disturb her. At times like that, I would like to be stronger, to have a protective shell to keep me safe all my life. Then nothing could ever hurt me.

———

The whole neighborhood went to Aziz's wedding. They held it in this big reception room in Livry-Gargan with a real orchestra from Fez that came over just for this occasion. Aziz hired two *négafas*, married women in charge of organizing the party: decorations, clothes, makeup, the bride's jewelry, food, all that kind of stuff. It was a big grand wedding all right. Aziz really put on a show. Anyway, that's what I heard, because, in the end, we weren't invited.

We don't see that social worker Mme DuDoodad anymore because she's on maternity leave. She said she'll be back after her baby's born. It annoyed me when she said that, because it sounded like: "No matter what, in a year you'll still be poor, you'll still need me." Worse, while we're waiting for her to come back, we're stuck with this shady replacement. She's always got her eyes half shut behind these massive bottle-bottom glasses with chunky pink frames. Plus, she talks very slowly in this scary voice, the kind of voice you can imagine saying: "I am Death! Follow me, it's your time!" But, fine, I'm not so bothered by all that. Don't give a shit, to be perfectly honest. The thing that gets me is that with her, I feel like Mom and me, we're just random numbers in her file. She does her job like an automaton. She could be a robot programmed to do this. I'm sure that if you scratched the skin on her back, if you really broke past the epidermis, you'd find an aluminium coating, some screws, and a serial number. I'm calling her Cyborg Services.

This week I'm not going to watch Sarah because her mom's on vacation and the two of them are going to Toulouse to Lila's sister's house. It's hard being separated from people who matter to you...

I'm thinking of Aunt Zohra and Youssef and some other people too...

Speaking of Aunt Zohra, she found the courage to tell her old crazy husband the whole story. Things got violent between them when he found out and the old wacko hit Aunt Zohra. He stopped after a minute because he'd had enough, his arms hurt too much, and he had heart palpitations. So he sat down and asked her for a glass of water to calm him. She went to get him his drink and that's how the whole thing ended...

She told us everything. Every day she prays to

God for her husband to go back to where he came from. And to think that only a little while ago, Mom was praying for that other man to come back.

These days I can see she's not so lost in her thoughts. She looks better. She's beginning to read a few words and she's so proud that she can write her first name without any mistakes. At first, she used to write *S* backward, like little kids do. It's true that from time to time I can see she's still anxious, like when she sits watching the turned-off TV. But it happens less often now. And also she's active and free to do anything she wants now while before that was definitely not the case. When Dad lived with us, there was no question about her working even though we were seriously broke. Because for Dad women weren't made for working in the outside world.

By the way, yesterday Hamoudi told me he'd found a job. He stumbled on this ad in that free paper *Paris Boum Boum*. This stereo-, video-, and computer-equipment rental company was looking for someone to do security. He called up right away, had an interview, and, bam, he was hired. Fine, he says it's kind of a pain because it's at night, but he's happy he's found real work, and it's better that way. He said he also feels like he's been hired to act like their guard dog, but he doesn't give a shit...

It makes me think of some of those houses in the Rousseau development where they put a sign up with a photo of a massive, supermenacing Doberman and a bubble that says BEWARE OF THE DOG!, while everyone knows that in the house is a toy poodle named Gramps who gets panic attacks from children and flies.

MONDAY, at Mme Burlaud's, it wasn't at all like normal. Right away when I got there, she told me to make myself comfortable and then she went out of the office saying: "I'll be right back!" like for the commercial breaks of variety shows. She didn't come back until twenty minutes later... and I noticed she smelled like alcohol. Real strong. Well, that really was nothing... During the session, I didn't have much to say so at one point she crossed her short little legs and went: "Maybe you've got a funny story to tell me?" At that moment I noticed she was wearing garters. I looked back and forth between her face and her garters and thought that this wasn't bad for a joke. Then she asked me thousands of questions

about Mom, nosy stuff about her love life and everything...I told her she didn't have one anymore since
he left. Mme Burlaud, she wanted to know if I could
see Mom making a new life with another man. Yeah,
I can see that. To tell you the truth, I'm planning it...

I watched a show about singles and new ways to
meet people. There's this thing called speed dating.
That means something is really fast. I know because
at Speed Burger, you order your hamburger and it's
ready in two minutes, plus it's 100 percent halal. Basically, these speed dates, they're like arranged meet-
ings. For seven minutes you sit facing somebody you
don't know. Just long enough to say: "I don't like
your face" or "Do you still live with your mom?"
Only I can't see Mom in a place like that. I don't
really believe she'll get together with someone again.
I was saying it just because I'd like her to, that's all.

Unless someone came directly to the house to ask
for her hand in marriage. Trouble is that now, she's
hardly ever home, apart from this month because her
training stops during summer vacation. I'm going to
stick up her office hours on the door like at the doctor's, with our requirements listed.

Alcoholics, old men, cowards need not apply.
Thank you in advance.

Preferably: Hard worker, cultured, witty, charming,
good teeth, stamp collector, and lover of canned,
peeled tomatoes.

Yeah, OK, I was kind of overly harsh with the old men part, but definitely no alcoholics. I never again want to have to wait outside Constantinois, the bar in the town square, so some man can finish knocking it back and I can take him home because he doesn't remember the way when he's drunk. Or prostituting my pride at the Sidi Mohamed Market buying cases of beer during Ramadan and lugging the empty bottles down to the recycling bins afterward. When the bottles smashed inside the bins, it made so much noise that everybody in our building knew how many bottles Dad had downed. With all the glass that was recycled thanks to him, he could have earned a merit of honor medal or become a mascot for the Green Party. I'd have given anything to trade my father for Tony Danza in *Who's the Boss?* but he was already taken. I don't think it's even possible now, with nothing to trade.

Hamoudi was really liking that job. And he was beginning to like living by the law. But they fired him because things were disappearing from the warehouse. At least six thousand euros worth of material and it was Hamoudi who got the blame. Not even his parents believed him when he denied it. They're convinced he's a good-for-nothing and keep telling him so.

Anyway, I believed him. "I don't give a shit, I'm clean, I've got nothing to be sorry for, I did a good job, and I didn't fall asleep once. Only thing they can hold against me is this filthy face..." He pointed to himself, eyes wide open. I didn't dare tell him he was handsome. I was scared he'd think something. Hamoudi, he's got really dark brown hair, clear enough skin, and big hazel eyes…A real Mediterranean man. He says that's why they unfairly accused him. I don't know if he's paranoid but, in any case, they had no right to accuse him without proof. That's no good.

Life is really full of disappointments. Coming home from the market this morning, I overheard two girls and a guy talking on the bus. The girls were twins, or nearly. They were dressed the same, had the same hairstyle, and they talked the same.

The guy was really little and he had his mouth open all the time. On the plus side, thank God, he didn't say anything. He just listened. The girls were chewing gum and blowing bubbles at the end of nearly every sentence.

"You know *The Pretender*?"

"Yeah sure!" (Bubble.)

"Do you watch it every day?" (Bubble.)

"Yeah!"

"You know the main character?"

"Right!" (Bubble.)

"His name is Jarod..." (Bubble.)

"Yeah! And he's seriously hot!"

"Well, I heard he's a homo!" (Bubble.)

"Serious? That's crazy! How do you know?" (Bubble.)

"My sister told me she saw it on the Internet."

"Oooh, that's so screwed up. I can't believe they're saying he's gay." (Bubble.)

Not Jarod. Someone could have said James Dean, Claude François, Michael Jackson, or Christian Morin, OK. But not Jarod. When I watched that series, I could never follow the story: He was the only reason I stayed crouched in front of the TV like an ass. Because he's really too hot. Those other gay guys out there are so lucky.

Mme Burlaud is always saying that all my life I'll get deceived and I've just got to get used to it. Yeah. But that wasn't written anywhere in my contract.

It's weird, but I can't stop thinking about that lameass Nabil and I still can't understand why he did that. Why he suddenly decided to glue his fat mouth to mine. And he's got enormous lips, I was scared he'd inhale me and I'd be a prisoner inside him. Once I got out of there, all the TV channels in the world would interrupt regular programming to get my eyewitness report of my stay in Nabil the loser. And then I would write a book called *Journey to the Center of Nabil.* It would definitely be a bestseller.

I wonder when he's coming back. Just to know. Oh yeah, and to tell him he's got some debts to pay back—and he has acne and pisses everyone off.

since мом's still on vacation until next week, we decided to hang around Paris together. It was actually the first time she'd seen the Eiffel Tower even though she's been living half an hour from it for almost twenty years. Before now, she only saw it on TV, on the one o'clock news on New Year's Day, when it's all lit up from top to bottom and people are partying, dancing, kissing, and getting wasted. Anyway, she was seriously impressed.

"It must be two or three times our building, yeah?"

I told her it had to be. But our building, and the projects in general, they don't get so much tourist interest. There aren't any Japanese hordes with their cameras standing at the bottom of the towers in the neighborhood. The only ones interested in us are the parasite journalists with their nasty reports on violence in the suburbs.

Mom, she would have been happy to stay there for hours looking at it. Me, I think it's ugly, but you can't deny it makes an impression because it's powerful: the Eiffel Tower. I'd like to have gone up in the red and yellow elevators that look like ketchup and mustard, but it was too expensive. And plus, we would have had to get in line behind the Germans, the Italians, the English, and piles of other tourists who aren't scared of heights and even less scared of spending their dough. We didn't have enough money to buy a miniature Eiffel Tower either, even uglier than the original, but still it's classy to have one on top of your TV. Tourist-trap stalls are crazy expensive. Plus, what those guys sell is total crap. Later, a pigeon took a shit on my shoulder. I tried wiping it off discreetly against a statue of Gustave Eiffel, 1832–1923, but the bird shit had gone hard and wouldn't come off. In the RER, people were staring at the stain and I felt serious *hchouma*. I felt kind of sick because it's the only jacket I have that doesn't look too ratty. If I wear any of the others, everybody calls me "Cosette" from *Les Misérables*. Anyway, I don't give a shit; whether it shows or not, I'll still be poor. Later, when my breasts are bigger and I'm a little bit more intelligent, like when I'm an adult, I'll join up with a group that helps people...

Knowing there are people who need you and you can be useful to them, it's really too cool.

One of these days, if I don't need my blood or one of my kidneys, I could donate them to the sick people who've had their names on the lists for forever. But, still, I wouldn't just do it for a clear conscience or so I could look at myself in the mirror when I'm taking off my makeup after work, but because I really wanted to do it.

Lila and Sarah are back from Toulouse and they brought me some little cakes. No doubt there's no connection between Toulouse and those cakes but it was a nice gesture I thought. Lila told me about how it went at her sister's. And then she talked a lot about herself, what her life was like before coming to the Paradise Estate, with Sarah's dad and everything...

Lila's from Algeria, like Aunt Zohra. She left her family early on to live the way she wanted, like in the novels she was reading at sixteen. She and Sarah's dad met very young and fell in love right away. Their story began like in those Sunday afternoon movies, with "I love you" every ten feet and never-ending walks on beautiful July days...

The problem was both families were against their being together. Sarah's dad's family, they're from Brittany since...I don't know...eighteen generations, while Lila's people, they're more the traditional Algerian family worried about preserving customs and religion. So they were all worked up about it from the start and then her ex-husband's family, they weren't so thrilled with her tan, if you know what I mean. The two of them decided to get married anyway, even though their relationship was already starting to fall apart. Lila says, looking back on it, she realizes they did it more out of rebellion than love. Plus, her wedding day is still a nightmare of a bad memory. Atmosphere like death, hardly any guests on her side, and, as if by chance, lots of pork in the meal her father-in-law cooked. And who knew if he put it in the wedding cake too, just to screw with her.

He was always dying of laughter from his own taste-
less jokes about religion. At every family meal—at
least the ones she was invited to—at 7:45 out came
the atheist joke. And Lila already felt out of place...

And then one day she'd had enough—of her
father-in-law's jokes, of cured sausage for an appe-
tizer, and of her permanently unemployed husband
who spent all his time slumped on the couch gawking
at repeats on the TV and drinking cheap beer. So she
asked for a divorce and it hasn't been easy. These
days she's bringing up her little girl all by herself, but
she's still hoping to meet someone who "fits" her perfectly. It made me think of an article about single
moms I read in a magazine lying on the coffee table
at the doctor's. In any case, I've figured out that behind that front of a supermarket cashier who cuts
out trendy articles from *Mademoiselle*, Lila's a big
dreamer.

And maybe there's something to what women's
magazines say about the perfect man, after all. They
have these three-page articles explaining how the
right guy, meaning the one for you, is never far away,
but often you don't realize it right away. There was
the first-person account from Simone, thirty-nine,

telling how her ex-neighbor from across the hall, Raymond, fell in love with her from day one. At first she didn't look at him at all, and now he's the man of her life. They're married and have two kids. That's how the story goes. They're happy because they've got a normal life and only have to go out once a week—to the supermarket.

For all I know, the perfect man I'm not even seeing and who I'll have two kids with later is Nabil...Before, I gave him a hard time, said the guy was a stain and stuff like that. But when I analyze the situation, I can see he helped me for months without getting anything in return, and most of all that he had the guts to kiss me by surprise and risk getting kneed right where it hurts. I'm sure if I asked Mme Burlaud her opinion, she'd tell me to give Nabil a chance. It's true he's not as bad as all that in the end. He's maybe even a good guy. And acne doesn't usually last your whole life.

When he gets back from vacation, I'm going to talk to him for real. Not play the autistic kid like I do with everyone else to protect myself. For all I know, maybe

I won't even need to say anything. It'll just happen just like in those romantic films where the leads don't talk to each other because they just understand each other straight off. I hope it'll be that way for Nabil and me. In any case it would work well for me…

I haven't talked about it with Mom yet but I think she likes Nabil because he's full of ambition. Like he wants to appear on *The Big Deal* and win the car. I admire that, because me, I just can't seem to see myself in the future. I should go for Shérif's technique: He's been putting money on the horses and playing the lottery for years and losing every time, but he just keeps on. He doesn't give a shit. Maybe that's the answer: Always keep a little hope and don't be scared of losing.

The news about samra has flooded the neighborhood. Samra's the prisoner who used to live in my building and whose brother and father pushed her to the edge until she had to get out. Somebody saw her a few days ago, not too far away. Or else very far away, I don't know anymore. Anyway, they're saying she ran away from home for a boy. I'm thinking she must have had an excellent reason to dare to escape from prison. It looks like she's doing fine and that she met this guy at that toy store La Grande Récré last December. She worked there over vacation, wrapping Christmas presents. She must have had some excellent technique and maybe that's what attracted her guy—he was working there too. According to what everyone's saying, he's a *toubab,* as in a whitey, a Camembert, an aspirin...So Samra's brother, who has a boxing glove for a brain, he wants this guy's skin when the only crime he's committed is giving a little love to his poor sister. I think they should have moved away and settled down farther out so people would leave them in peace. In a hideout, like runaways, totally guilty of doing something normal. Sometimes I think there are some people who have to fight for everything. It's a struggle even to love.

But good, now she's with the guy she loves, far away from that detention center that served as her home, and she can do what she wants. The main thing is that she's free, right. Well, more or less...It's just that he'd better not dump her. If after a year of being together, he suddenly tosses her stuff onto the landing, shouting: "Get out of my house!" she can't do anything except leave, without fighting back, resigned, like a fool...She would live in some pitiful hotel room that she'd pay for out of her ironing salary from the Farandole laundry. Most of all, she wouldn't believe in anything anymore. Not men, not love.

My wisdom teeth are coming in. It hurts crazy bad. I have to go and see Madame Atlan, the dentist around here. With her, you can't be scared. She's very friendly but she must have learned her job in the trenches, like during the Gulf War or the Turkish invasions, I don't know. Point is, she's kind of brutal, this lady. Once, she nearly ripped out my whole jawbone. I was trying to shout and wave my arms around in her chair so she could understand I was in pain, and she, all calm, keeps on going and says:

"You're a brave chick, come on, you can take it!"

Then since I was still in awful pain, she tried to take my mind off it:

"Do you like couscous balls?"

When she was a teenager, she must have had to choose between wrestler, riot cop, and dentist. It can't have been easy to decide, but she picked the one job out of the three that combines violence with perversity. No doubt it was more fun for a psychopath like her.

I can really picture her at my age, depressed teenager, a little bit masochist around the edges. She must have dressed like Action Man, listening to heavy metal to fall asleep at night and snacking on instant coffee powder by the teaspoon. And then one day, while buying a packet of rice at the supermarket, she falls in love with the old black American man in the photo on the orange box. He was called Uncle, this guy, and his family name was Ben's. Uncle Ben's, he's been on that package of rice for years, so he must have the record on being old. For all we know, he's been dead for years and nobody knows. Maybe Uncle's rice company hid his death from the whole world because they didn't want to disappoint thousands of customers. Poor Uncle, he may have died anonymously, all alone in the middle of a rice field. That makes me think of the kid in the Kinder egg photos. Goes back at least twenty years! Today the guy must be thirty, easy, a manager in a lavender toilet-deodorizer business, married to a stacked blond, and living in the United States in one of those trendy suburbs where the houses all look the same with a swimming pool and the Jeep parked in front. And best is the dog that doesn't bite, yeah, him again, all well-behaved in his kennel with his name written above: Walker.

I wonder why they're called wisdom teeth... The more they grow, the more things you learn? Me, I've learned that it hurts to learn.

THis one, I have to say I wasn't expecting it at all. Sarah's the one who told me everything. If she weren't four years old, I'd never have believed it. So while I was reading one of Lila's magazines, she plopped in front of me, looked at me in her "I-know-something-you-don't-know" way and said:

"So Mommy's in love with that big man who has gross teeth."

Lila and Hamoudi! I thought I was going to have an asthma attack. How could they have done that to me? I felt like I was in a TF1 report, on that show *Seven to Eight* presented by TV's own Brainy Ken and Smart Barbie.

It starts like this:

Fifteen, and disenchanted already. For her, life is just a brief illusion. From birth, she is an enormous disappointment to her parents, particularly her father, who was expecting a little boy to come out of his wife's belly, weighing in at seven and a half pounds, measuring twenty inches, equipped with a thingy of average size, perhaps he wanted a boy to reinforce his own virility.

Alas, so goes life's drama, he brought into the world a little girl already wondering what the hell she was doing there…

Then you see me appear on the screen, my face blurred out and my voice disguised, like a cartoon. I turn to the camera and start pouring my heart out:

Anyway, I mean, what's the point of living? I still don't have breasts, my favorite actor is gay, there are pointless wars and inequality between people. And now the cherry on top: Hamoudi's fooling around with Lila and he hasn't said a word about it to me. Yeah… I'm right, our lives are shit.

Then, the guy doing the voice-over takes the lead again, with all this really tearjerker music in the background.

The kid's not wrong... It's true, our lives are shit. I think I'm going to stop doing voice-overs for TV. It's a crappy career, you never get any recognition for what you do, meaning nobody ever asks for your autograph in the street, it doesn't make you a celebrity, it's a fool's career. I'll set up a group: Voice-overs Anonymous, *because no one ever reads my name in the credits at the end of the show. I've had enough, I'm over this...*

But while I'm still on air, I'd like to take this opportunity to let you know I'm selling my car if anyone's interested, it's a green Twingo in good condition, practically new, only seven years old...

And to find that out from Sarah... I mean, what's next? Why didn't Hamoudi say anything to me? He still takes me for a kid? Maybe he thinks I don't understand this kind of stuff? I've been able to understand stuff a lot more complicated. I've always filled out all the paperwork for Mom, and even when my dad was around, it was me who did it. Even when I'd had enough, because tax forms are like gobbledy-gook. Once, I asked my dad how he and Mom managed before I could read and write. He thought I was being a smartass. He hit me. And not just a little. He hit me hard for a long time. But I never cried. At least, not in front of him, because my dad was like Hamoudi's: He thought girls were weak, that they were made for crying and doing the dishes.

Luckily not all dads are like that. Take Nabil's, he's nice. He has never hit him and he talks to him all the time. They even go out for walks together when the weather's nice. He's lucky, Nabil: His parents are cultured, they can read and write, and for his thirteenth birthday they bought him these kick-ass Rollerblades I've dreamed about all my life. I used to cut pictures of them out of the Christmas catalogs so I could get a closer look.

Hamoudi didn't get it at all. I'm not a kid anymore.

мme вuяlɑud's ʂoʈ ɑ ρoiɴʈ: With time, lots of things change. Sometimes I think she should have gone into Chinese proverbs for a career. She was saying this about Mom, who found a new job thanks to her training. When she told me, she had this happy look on her face and it's been forever since that happened. She's a cafeteria lady for the city. She serves the kids at the Jean-Moulin elementary school. She even has her name written in pink on her shirt: Yasmina.

There's just one thing that bugs her: At the cafeteria, especially on Tuesdays, she serves pork and she thinks she's going to hell because of it. She made a big confession to me. She told me that the *haâlouf*—that's pig to you and me—looked surprisingly tasty... That cracked me up. But she felt way guilty for daring to think that and for telling me.

I don't know what they did to her in that course but she's not the same. She's happier, more radiant. That's what they said in *Paris-Match* magazine about Céline Dion, right after the birth of her baby René-Charles. And she's starting to get by better in reading too. She reads the syllables more correctly now. All of a sudden, she'll stop in the street to work out what's written on billboards or shop signs. The other day, she even bought the newspaper. Yeah, OK, so it was *Charlie-Hebdo*—that political cartoon magazine—because it's got lots of pictures, but it's a start...Even Cyborg Services noticed she was making progress.

I mention her because she came over to the house the other day, sort of unexpectedly. She asked lots of questions about Mom's work, then she started talking about my sense of purpose and my future in hairdressing. What did she think? That playing around with people's hair was my big passion in life? What a ***** (I'm doing some self-censoring here)! She didn't underline the positive sentences in our stupid twelve-

digit file. She still doesn't understand it was hairdressing or nothing. Fool. At one point, she thought she
was being really smart, and looked at me and said:

"It's too easy not to choose and to let others decide
for you, Doria..."

That's when I broke out my best imitation of the
Hollywood film star. I stared straight into her eyes
and said with emotion in my voice and tears in the
corners of my eyes:

"Are you sure about that?"

That knocked you off balance, didn't it, Miss Cyborg
Services? After that she didn't have anything to say, so
she started talking about the war in Iraq with Mom.

"It's always the women and children who suffer,
especially in war. It's horrible! Hmm...Right. By the
way, I hear you've managed to pay the rent on time
this month?"

Still feeling queen bee, I went into the kitchen to
clean the gas burners before Cyborg did her inspection, because they were truly disgusting.

Maybe that's what I should do. Acting. Making films is
class, right. I'll have glory, money, big prizes...I can

see myself already at the Cannes festival, striking a pose and smiling at the herd of flashing photographers, dressed like Sissi in that fifties film *Sissi impératrice*. In some casual motion, I'd salute the crowd that had come to cheer for me. Because all those people, they'd be there for me, not for Nicole Kidman, Julia Roberts... No, just for me. And Mom, all choked up, interviewed by the TV networks: "Iz a looong time I dream of my dotter climbing ze staircase at Cannes, iz woonderfool, zank you very much..." Not the staircase, Mom, the steps... While I'm walking up them, I'd be secretly hoping the ceremony would be broadcast on Moroccan television and that my father the Beard would just happen to see it. He'd be spitting his own nails for leaving because now his daughter's a star. Not a peasant woman. During the awards ceremony in the great room at the Palais, in the front row I'd see my mom, Hamoudi, pregnant Lila, Sarah, and Mme Burlaud. Robert De Niro would call out my name to present me with the prize for best actress. That player would make the most of it by kissing me and sneaky-like slipping his cell number into my cleavage. Everyone's on their feet. Me, in front of all those people. Standing ovation! Thinking ahead, I've written a brilliant speech. And, just to feel more comfortable, more natural, more me, right, I've learned it by heart:

"...and finally, I'd like to thank the social services office in Seine-Saint-Denis for sponsoring my trip to Cannes...Thank you, oh dear fans!"

That's not all. But I realize, instead of daydreaming, I'd be better off putting more energy into scrubbing this freaking stove because it's still totally scuzzy. They piss me off with their surprise visits.

Our dear Cyborg Services, after doing her nice little inspection, left the apartment.

We thought that was it. Cut. Wrap for the day. Everyone clear the set. But no. Fifteen minutes later she's back again, out of breath because she's hoofed it up all those stairs—the elevator's still out of order—and is completely panicked. She explained how someone just jacked her Opel Vectra, which she'd parked in front of our building. She'd come back up to our place to call a taxi. Kind of stunned, Mom said: "But, madame, our telephone iz cut off two or three months ago..." That social worker, I swear, it looked for sure like she'd seen the devil: "But that's not written in your file..."

The other evening, I saw Hamoudi and he told me about his deal with Lila. At first I wanted to have a serious grown-up conversation with him about the fact that he didn't tell me anything... But in the end, I didn't dare say a word. He looked so in love. I didn't want to break him out of the spell. He talked about nothing but her for two hours. Lila's replaced Rimbaud. He's shown the poet the door. Go on, out, skip it... He's even planning to take her on a weekend trip with his drug money.

Then he started talking about fate. That again. In any case, here everything's linked to fate. For better or worse. And me, I'm realizing fate doesn't like me so much right now. Like Mme Burlaud says, I haven't finished being disappointed yet. She's worse than insightful, this lady, she's got super x-ray vision. It's true: She said that to me before summer break. The result? I spend my whole summer banging my head against a brick wall.

So seeing how I have nothing to lose, I decided to prepare myself psychologically for Nabil's return. I was really expecting a sensational event, like a movie: *Nabil, The Return 2.* Yeah, that's it, Nabil's return. Nabil, the fat lame-o.

I told myself that when he got back, I'd be able to tell him how my feelings were all muddled up and heavy inside me. Meaning I was ready, right...And him, that little acne-faced ass, he gets back from vacation all tan and doesn't know me anymore. Yeah, ever since Nabil got back from Djerba, I don't rate with him. He walks right past me without even saying hello. And he's got an earring and some whiskers on his chin now. He grew up, he's showing off, here we go.

It makes me think of that movie *Grease* with Olivia Newton John and John Travolta. In that story, it's summer. Olivia and Trav really dig each other, as in *kiffer,* right. They run along the beach, sing happy songs, and kiss on the lips over by the rocks. Then school starts again, and Olivia's still feeling all *kiffe*-d up, but Trav, to show off in front of his crew at school, he doesn't look at her anymore because he's ashamed of her. He totally laughs in her face. And she, like a fool with her ponytail and pink dress, runs off to bawl her eyes out. Weak woman. But the real bastard's Trav, with his tight black leather pants and cartoon haircut. When I told Mme Burlaud the whole story about Nabil on Monday, she cheered me up real good. Without even meaning to…

"Maybe Nabil prefers boys. Had you thought about that?"

Oh yeaaaah…Like Jarod. Maybe that's it. A mother like his, that could turn a boy gay, couldn't it? If it's true, he probably knows all Madonna's songs by heart and wears tight underwear.

Psssh…Whatever. Actually, Mme Burlaud hasn't got a clue if Nabil's gay or not. Me, all I know is I'm kind of disappointed because I thought he really liked me, that's all…

our neighbor Rachida, the biggest gossip in the projects, came to the house the other night. She brought us thirty euros and some groceries for the week. From time to time, people from the area give us donations and it kind of helps us out. But what's good about big Rachida is that as well as giving us charity, she gives us "Celebrity Gossip," the Paradise Estate remix. She's the one who brings us the latest news and when she's got an especially juicy piece of gossip, she's as proud of it as if it were her firstborn son.

Rachida talked to Mom again about Samra, the prisoner of the tenth floor, the one who ran away from home to be with her guy. It seems she actually got married to him.

Samra's dad, a retired torturer now that his daughter left, one morning while buying the paper, happens to turn to the "Congratulations to Young Couples" column and there's his daughter's last name, and so his last name, right next to the *toubab* guy's. The old guy couldn't take it and fell sick, they said part of his body was paralyzed. It had to be the shock of seeing his name "dirtied" like that. The name his father, his grandfather, and others before them had borne. Another question of honor, I guess...

Samra's dad's going to paralyze the other half of his body the day he happens to land on the "Welcome Newborns" column in the paper. If he could put his pride aside, he'd see that the most important thing is his daughter's happiness. (I'm using American TV series morality but I don't care, I'm cool with that.)

And with all these stories about fate, I'm starting to think there's no such thing as chance.

It's all bullshit. It's not luck if Passe-Partout, the midget in that game show *Fort Boyard,* turns out to be a civil servant working for the RATP in real life and his name's actually André Bouchet. You shit a brick the day you're fare-hopping at the Gare du Nord and then there's some tiny inspector asking to see your ticket, and you don't see anybody at first, but then you look down and see Passe-Partout. Plus, you know there's no point trying to skip it, because the guy runs crazy fast, I've seen him on the *Fort*. For all we know, maybe all the guys from the show are civil servants in real life. Imagine Dad Fouras as a cop? I'm telling you, if they cut off our TV like they did with the phone, it will be too much. It's all I have. When we did the Middle Ages with M. Werbert, my geography teacher from last year, he told us the church used stained-glass windows as the poor person's Bible, for people who couldn't read. For me, TV today is like the poor person's Koran.

When I watch TV, Mom listens to Enrico Macias and knits. Oh yeah. Forgot about that, she's started knitting again. She used to do it a lot before Dad took off. Now she knits at home with "Jéquiline," as in Jacqueline, the teacher she's now friends with. Jacqueline was blond before she was old and gray. She told me. Some Sundays she makes rhubarb jam and her neighbors are soccer fans, so on game nights she has problems getting to sleep. She's nice, Jacqueline. Once, Mom told Jacqueline she needed a waxed tablecloth, just like that in the middle of a conversation, and the next week, Jacqueline brought a waxed tablecloth over to the house. Yeah, OK, so it was pretty ugly. There were these hunting scenes, with big stags and lots of Bambis getting shot at...But I thought it was nice of her, all the same.

And another thing, Jacqueline's interested in bunches of stuff. She asks Mom questions about religion, Moroccan culture, and lots of other things like that... "It's so I know if what they're saying on the TV is true...you know..."

And sometimes she tells Mom stories from the Bible. The other day, she told her the story of Job. I remember one time we read an extract in our French class with Madame Jacques. She shouted at me because when it was my turn to read, instead of pronouncing it Job-rhymes-with-globe, I said "Jahb." Like what they call your work in America or the name of the fat guy in *Star Wars*. And that crazy old bag of a Mme Jacques accused me of "sullying our beautiful language" and other stuff just as stupid.

Nothing I can do, I didn't know even know this Job guy existed. "It's the faaaaulttt of people like yooouu that our Frrrench herrrrritttage is in a coma!"

Thanks to Lila, Hamoudi's come through his bad spell. He's got a new job: security at Malistar, the mini-market under our building. But it's just for now while he's waiting to find something else and then quit dealing for good. He's smoking a lot less. We see each other less too. But he's better and that's the most important thing. He's the one who was always saying how it was all fucked anyway, there was no way out. But when he said that, he'd always apologize right away after.

"I've got no right to say things like that to a fifteen-year-old kid. You can't listen to me, understand? You've got to believe! OK?"

It was sort of like a threat. But he was right. He's found his emergency exit, now. He talks seriously about making a life with Lila. That means there isn't just rap and soccer. Love's another way to get out of this mess.

The first day back at school is one of the worst days of the year along with Christmas. I had diarrhea for three days beforehand. The idea of going to a new school you don't know, with lots of people you don't know and, worse, who don't know you either, well, it gives me the shits. Sorry, upset stomach. That sounds less disgusting.

Lycée Louis-Blanc. Who is this guy anyway? Louis Blanc? I looked it up. With a name like that, he just had to be in the dictionary of proper names.

"Louis BLANC (1811–1882). Journalist and socialist activist."

In France, being described with three words end-

ing in "ist" is all you need for them to name a school,
a street, a library, or a metro station after you. I
thought it might be a good idea to do a little research,
you never know when a thug might ask me: "Hey!
You there! Who's Louis Blanc?" Then I'd look the
dumbass straight in the eye and I'd say to that sandpit
of a scumbag who thought he was scaring me: "Journalist, socialist, activist..." And with an American
accent too, like in those films we used to watch in English class. That shut you up, right? Even if you're
not circumcised, clown.

The morning of the first day back, Mom was too
cute. She wanted her daughter to be the most beautiful for "Ze new skool, the *jdida*..." The new place.
"Hamdoullah..." Thanks be to God. She ironed my
least ugly clothes, especially the fake Levi's jeans
(very good imitation) she picked up for me at La
Courneuve market. "Coooome on, ladies 'n' gents,
it's too good to be true! Just too good to be true!
We're *giving* them away, Levi's jeans at twelve euros!
They're seventy in the stores! It really is just too good
to be true! Get 'em while stocks last! Cooooome and

get 'em!" She fixed up my long black hair. Hers was
just like it when she was younger. After, as she got
older, she lost some of it and it wasn't all black anymore. She did my hair up in a ponytail, after she'd
brushed it with olive oil. That's old-school hairdressing. Like they do in the *bled*. Me, I don't like it so
much, but I didn't say anything to her because she
was too happy making me all pretty. It reminded me
of the mornings we had class photos at elementary
school and she used to do the same thing. My hair
was all silky and shiny in those photos, like in the
Schwarzkopf ads: "Professional quality care for your
hair." But actually, it was greasy and smelled of food
fried in Zit Zitoun olive oil. When the teacher patted
me on the head for giving a good answer, she'd wipe
her hands on her jeans. On class picture day, all the
teachers wore jeans.

I don't care. For a little while I was pretty in Mom's
eyes. When people say I look like her, I get proud. I
hardly look anything like my dad at all. Except my
eyes, which are green like his. In my father's eyes,
there was always some nostalgia. So when I look at
myself in the mirror, I see him and his nostalgia too.

All the time. Mme Burlaud told me I'll be completely cured the day I see me in the mirror. Just me.

So that people see my eyes better, Mom drew around them with liner. She kissed me on the forehead and closed the door, asking that God go with me. I hope he's got his own ride because public transport, man, it stresses me out. I walked down to city hall to catch the bus to Louis-Blanc. And there, in the bus, who do I see spread out across four seats, Walkman jammed into his ears? Nabil the loser. Some luck.

Our eyes cross paths and, like in the movies, he makes this guy-full-of-guilt face. He struggles to nod his head and gives me this tiny... "Uh, how y'don?" So now he's being a lazybones too. Too annoying and bored to pronounce the letters *O* and *U* and *I* and *G*? My answer's to screw up my eyes and pinch my lips really tight, so he gets: "I'm over you, Nabil the fat bastard, you pizza-faced microbe, homosexual, and total ego-trip." Hope he knew how to translate all that.

Then I went and sat next to an old African man holding these wooden prayer beads in his hand. He was turning the beads slowly through his fingers.

Reminded me of my dad in his rare moments of piety, even if he was nothing like a good Muslim. You don't pray after demolishing a pack of Kronenbourg 1664. There's no point.

So, anyway, Nabil got out three stops before me. He didn't say good-bye, or see you, or *beslama*. Nothing, *walou*. It must have already taken it out of him saying: "How y'don?" Not even a real "How are you?" So "see you" was too much to ask. I admit that pissed me off so much I was feeling some hate. But the worst was to come.

I got to the lycée louis-blanc, man of the proper-name dictionary, and found myself in the middle of thirty bleach-blond bitches with big perms. It was all liberty, equality, fraternity. It didn't look like the first day of school. It felt more like a casting call. They were all so decked out, sporting "the look," as they say on TV. And there's me with my kohl eyeliner and fake jeans. I didn't exactly feel with it.

Then they called us up by group to go to our classrooms. Our principal's a woman. Her name's Agnès Bernard, but there's no connection to the designer Agnès B. She's a young teacher, barely thirty, blond, who talks with a lisp and dresses kind of like the students. Yeah, she's common. Lucky she talks funny, or else there'd be nothing original about her at all, poor thing. She explained what the hairdressing certificate program involved and what the hell we were going to be doing all year. "Product technology: regulation of personal hygiene products, primary ingredients used in hair-care products... Equipment technology: instruments for drying and styling the hair, cutting tools and implements, styling accessories... Professional techniques, of course: shampooing, bleaching, coloring, perms, drying, styling..." She might as well be speaking Chinese, right? Cracked-out Chinese. What the hell was I going to do in that place?

By the time I got home, I was seriously depressed. I don't like busting into tears but I couldn't help myself anymore. I was hardly through the front door when I started blubbering. I'm surprised I didn't set off an emergency flood alert in the building. Luckily Mom wasn't there. I know her, she'd have started blubbering too without even knowing why I was blubbering.

A few days later, I stopped babysitting. I've been too busy, busy doing lots of stuff. Completely overbooked. No more time to spend worrying over a kid. Sorry.

Nah, I don't watch Sarah anymore because Hamoudi's doing it now instead of me. Since he works in the complex and finishes at four o'clock, he can pick the little one up. It's cool. Yeah. Plus, it makes them like a real family.

I saw Hamoudi when I went shopping downstairs. He talked to me in front of Malistar while he unloaded some boxes of rice. After about five minutes I felt like I was bugging him, so I headed out. I have to say, he talks to me like everybody else now. He's not Hamoudi from number 32 anymore. And he knows it. The other day, I found a note in my mailbox, along with a twenty-euro bill. It was signed "Moudi." A nickname. A shitty nickname. I could have definitely come up with something better. And when I think how Hamoudi used to say he thought nicknames were ridiculous. And here he is signing as "Moudi." Lila could at least have found something more interesting. Moudi. Moody...schmoody...doody...what? Doesn't mean anything, doesn't say anything. He doesn't say anything either, not anymore. Nicknames are so bourgeois: "Do you want some more rabbit, my little duck?" That line works the other way around too. How sad is that?

So long story short, he wanted to clear his conscience because he felt guilty for kind of having dropped me, so he put this note in the mailbox along with twenty euros. He thinks money can fill a hole or what? He's got to stop reading the psychobabble cases in those women's magazines on Lila's coffee table. Even what he wrote was nonsense: "If you need me, you know where to find me..." Yeah, and, well, what I know, Hamoudi, is you're not over at number 32 anymore. You've dropped us, Rimbaud and me. You traitor. All the same in every way. Traitors.

And even Mme Burlaud. If she wasn't paid to see me at a set time once a week, I'm sure she'd have cut me loose by now.

walking past the bar in the center of town, I noticed a piece of paper stuck up in the window. It said: "LOTTO WINNER HERE: 65,000 EUROS." They always write "WINNER HERE," but they never put who it is. The guys who work at the bar-tabac are good people. They aren't snitches. They'd never name names. Except this time, I know who it is, the lucky bastard to hit the jackpot. It's our very own international Shérif. He's definitely going to have to go on TV and become famous. That way, he'll get around the identity checks. Yeah, if he's a big shot, no one will need to ask for his name or I.D. anymore. Still, he deserved it. He's been gambling for so long. I'm kind of curious to know what he'll do with the money. Change his baseball cap? Jeans? Apartment? Neighborhood? Country? Maybe he'll buy a villa in Tunisia, settle down over there and find himself a wife who's a genius with couscous...

Hey, speaking of marriage, I grilled my mom on it. She's in love with the mayor of Paris. She likes, no, she kiffes, Bertrand Delanoë ever since she saw him on TV laying the memorial plaque at Saint-Michel. It was in honor of the Algerians thrown into the Seine during the demonstration on October 17, 1961. I borrowed books about it from the Livry-Gargan library.

Mom thought it was really good and big of Bertrand to do something in memory of the Algerian people. Very dignified, very classy. Now that she's single, I'm thinking of giving Bertrand Delanoë a call. A big poster campaign with Mom's photo (the black-and-white one in her passport) and below, the slogan: "I kiffe you for real, Monsieur Mayor, call me..." It'll drive Bertrand wild if he sees the poster. Plus, I think he's single too. It's true, you never see him out on the town with chicks. And Mom, she's like a trifecta: "You can win it all." She cooks, she cleans, and she even knits. I bet nobody's ever knitted a pair of wool boxers before for "M. the Mayor, I have the honor to inform you that..." He'll be way happy about those come winter.

The other night, I ran into Hamoudi by the recycling bins. He told me he was just looking for me. Pffffff. That's so not true. I could easily see he was headed for Lila's.

"Hamoudi, what a liar!"

No, actually, I didn't say that. I just said: "Oh, cool..." We talked for a little while. He told me he was sorry he's not around as much as he used to be... Big picture is, he made me see he's got a new life now and I also got the message I wasn't really part of it anymore.

"Hamoudi, I liked you better when you were a ghetto thug and gave the finger to all the keepers of the peace."

No, I didn't really say that. I just said: "Yeah, OK."

Lila and Hamoudi are even making marriage plans. His mom must be happy. She'll have managed to marry off all her children. "Final level reached. Bonus. You're a winner." The old lady's completed her mission. And it came at just the right time. Twenty-eight's fine, it's right before his mom starts asking questions... "Allah, my God, perhaps my son he iz a... maggot?! *Hchouma*..."

Hamoudi had better invite me to his wedding. If he doesn't, I'll turn him over to the Five-o... No, I'm joking. That's too far. There's this guy in the neighborhood who turned in his boys to the cops. Ever since, he's been persecuted and the guys in the projects call him "the harki," aka an Algerian who fought for France, a deserter. Me, I'm not that low. Poor guy, his turncoat rep is going to follow him as long as he's on the Paradise Estate. Here, you just have to do one thing that's not so cool and it's all over for you. You get pigeonholed until you die.

It reminds me of the story of a girl who lived around here a few years back. They even wrote about her in the newspaper. She was a good student in school, everybody in the neighborhood respected her family, and the kids from the center of town, known to be real tough crews, would even help her dad with his shopping bags when he came back from the market on Sunday mornings. This girl was in a theater group funded by the Livry-Gargan town council and her parents let her follow her passion no problem. Sometimes they even went to see her performing in the end-of-year show. So, basically, things weren't going too badly for her, even if her parents did think these activities were just a hobby, like painting on Wednesday afternoons at the rec center when you're in nursery school. But this girl, she really loved to act and wanted to make a career out of it. When she was eighteen, she even performed in different towns across France with her company.

Then one day her parents found an anonymous letter in their mailbox. The whole thing was published in that antiracist city paper *Friend to Friend*, together with a first-person account by this girl:

> *Your daughter keeps the wrong kind of company. She goes out a lot and is often seen walking with boys. We've heard things about her that dirty your name and your good reputation. The whole neighborhood knows that **** hangs around with young men and that she is forgetting the right path. God says that you are responsible for the path of your children. You must be strict with her so that she fears her family and the religion of Islam. Now people and men see*

*that your daughter is from the street and that she is
not afraid. The French are taking her on the road to
evil. We have noticed that she wears makeup, that
she dyes her hair. This means she likes to please
men and that she is tempting Satan. If something
shameful happens, God will see you have been too
free with her and you are as much to blame as she is.*

*God offers mercy and clemency. She can return to
the family and to our customs if you apply harsh
measures. Prayer can be a hand from God for those
who turn away from the path.*

*Your family is one that we respect and it must
continue that way. A girl can be put on the right path
by her father. You must believe in the power God
entrusts you with to be a good family.*

After the letter, everything changed for this girl.
The anonymous bastard who wrote all that stupid
stuff managed to convince her parents. They felt
guilty for giving their daughter "too much" freedom. So, all of a sudden, she wasn't allowed to do
theater anymore. Or go out, not even to buy bread.
Most of all, she started hearing talk of marriage. The

last resort when parents feel their daughters slipping through their fingers.

Then in *Friend to Friend*, she wrote in about how she decided to run away from home. Today, she lives on her own and hardly has any contact with her parents. But she's with the Comédie-Française and she's earning a living doing what she loves. She won after all.

тнеɾе you нαve iт. I'm sixteen. Sixteen springs, as they say in the movies. Nobody remembered. Not even Mom. No one wished me a happy birthday this year. Same thing happened last year... Oh wait. Last year I got a gift certificate from Agnès B. with a special free gift if I sent back the "Agnès B. wishes you a happy birthday" voucher within ten days. But this year I got nothing. Even Agnès B. hates me. She's got a grudge because I didn't send her crappy voucher back last time. Fool. I don't give a shit. Anyway, their gifts are always bigger in the photo than in real life.

If no one remembered my birthday this year, too bad.

And to be honest, I kind of understand. I'm no one special. Some people, everyone remembers their birthdays. Some are even on the calendar in the paper. But me, I'm nobody. And I don't know how to do anything big. Well, yeah, I can do a few things, but nothing special, really: I can crack my toes, send a string of saliva out of my mouth and suck it back in again, do an Italian accent in front of the bathroom mirror in the morning... Yeah, I can get by without much trouble in the end. But if I was a boy, maybe it would be different... It would definitely be different.

For a start, my father would still be here. He wouldn't have gone back to Morocco. And for Christmas 1994, I would have definitely gotten Fisher-Price Rollerblades and a reply to the letter I sent Santa Claus. Yeah, it would all have gone better if I'd been a guy. I would have lots of photos of me as a little kid, like little Sarah. My dad would have taught me to chew tobacco. He'd have told me plenty of scandalous stories he'd picked up on building sites and plus, from time to time, he'd even have patted me on the shoulder, a sort of bonding, conspiracy thing, like: "You're a good guy!" Yeah, yeah. I would even have had fun scratching myself between the legs a lot to prove my virility. I would have really liked to have been a boy. But fine, I'm a girl. A broad. A chick. A babe, even. I'll get used to it eventually.

The other day Mom and me, we went to the Taxiphone in the square to call Aunt Zohra. More and more of these Taxiphones are popping up everywhere. With their wooden booths, glass doors, and phone numbers on the handsets, they remind me of Morocco. Basically, the whole Taxiphone idea is made in the *bled*. The one in the square is like having a little bit of Oujda in Livry-Gargan.

Aunt Zohra's doing well. She promised to come and visit us soon. And she said that Youssef gets out in May. It sounded definite because she didn't even say "inshallah." It seems that, bit by bit, with each visit she recognizes him less and less. She told Mom he's starting to rant in this really extreme way, even worse than his dad. With that comparison, I'm thinking it must be bad.

He must have met some weird people in the slammer. Youssef was always easygoing before and way more open than most guys his age... These days, he talks about grave sins and divine punishments. Before, he didn't really give a shit about all that. He even bought bacon-flavored chips on the sly just to find out what they tasted like. I think it's shady, this kind of supersudden change. Someone must have taken advantage of him being vulnerable in prison and inserted some big fat disks into his brain. Thank God he gets out in May.

For good news, I landed on this regional news report on France 3 the other evening and who do I see on the screen all styling in her pink *boubou*, Miss Africa dress? Fatouma Konaré, my mom's ex-coworker from the Formula 1 in Bagnolet. Her name was up on the screen with, underneath it: "Union delegate." The commentary said the girls had won their battle. Their demands would be met shortly. Even the employees who got fired during the strike as well as those who left without any compensation are going to see reparations for their losses. Does that mean Mom'll see some money too, even if she didn't go on strike? Right away, I started thinking about that fat jerk M. Winner. He must have been left sitting there scratching himself! Ha! Well done.

And so there you go, that'll do for my birthday present, knowing there is some justice in this world after all. I was starting to seriously doubt it. I was fed up with always hearing: "The wheel will come around." I don't see what wheel they're talking about and, well, it's a stupid expression.

With all the events of this year, I was thinking that, frankly, life's too unfair. But now just recently, I've changed my mind a bit...Lots of things have happened that have changed my point of view. Like that guy who was wrongly imprisoned, Patrick Dils, appearing on that show *Everybody's Talking About It*. And the cleaners' situation at the Formula 1 in Bagnolet. And Hamoudi and Lila getting married next April. And one last thing, the way Mom's changed in a year. Seeing her getting better every day, fighting for both of us to live, has started me thinking it'll all work out and maybe I'll be lucky and be like her.

At work, I'm taking after her because going for a hairdressing certificate gives no rest. Drying, styling, and when you're finished, well, start all over again. No break. Even God had a rest on the seventh day. It's not normal. The one thing that comforts me is that I'm coping all right with school this year. Note: If I'd been useless in a hairdressing class, then I really would be worried.

MME BURLAUD told me my therapy was finished. I asked if she was sure. She laughed. That means I'm doing well. Or else she's had enough of my stories. She must be flipping her lid with all the stuff I tell her.

I'm glad it's stopping because there were some things that bugged me about her. Her name, for starters...Burlaud, I mean seriously, that name doesn't go with anything, plus it sounds ugly. Then there's her perfume that stinks like RID and those crazy tests to find out stuff about me...And, also, she's old. She comes from another time. I see it when

I'm talking to her, I have to pay attention to everything I'm saying. Can't say a single word in street
slang or anything casual, even if it's the best way of
getting her to understand how I'm feeling...When
I can't find the right phrase and I say something
like "trippin'" or "shady," she takes it to mean something else or she does her spesh face. Doing her spesh
face means looking like a total idiot, because spesh
(special-ed) classes at elementary school were for the
slowest kids, the ones with the biggest problems. So
you say spesh for someone who's kind of stupid, you
know...

Mme Burlaud and me weren't always on the same
wavelength. That said, I know it's thanks to all this
I'm doing better. I don't deny she helped me big time.
Hey, I even said thank you to Mme Burlaud. A real
thank you.

But as she was leaving she said something that
seemed strange to me: "Good luck!" I'm used to
hearing: "See you next Monday!" But this time she
says: "Good luck." It reminded me of the first time I
rode a bike without training wheels.

Once, Youssef lent me his bike. He had told me
he'd push me while I was pedaling, and then at one

point, when I wasn't expecting it, he said: "I let go!"
His voice was far away. He'd let go a while back. And
I kept on pedaling. Mme Burlaud's "good luck" had
the same effect on me as Youssef's "I let go!" So it
goes. She's let me go.

Leaving, I felt a little like in the scene-before-the-
end in a film, when the heroes have kind of solved the
problem and it's time to construct a conclusion. Except for me, my conclusion, it's going to be longer
and harder than the one in *Jurassic Park*.

For example, I still don't know what I really want
to do in life. Because hairdressing, let's say it's something you do while you're waiting for something else
to come along. A little like Christian Morin. He was
the host of *Wheel of Fortune* for years, but his real
calling was the clarinet...

Yesterday, I got an unexpected visit. Nabil the loser came over to my place while Mom was out. I opened the door. He was there, leaning against the wall, recently shaved and smelling good. He took off his baseball cap, smiled at me, and said:

"Hi, how's it going?"

I spent a quarter of a century staring at him and not saying anything, as shocked as those people who win the Casino supermarket annual lottery draw. Then, after a quick moment of serious reflection, I decided I could let him in. We went to sit down and we talked. About his vacation in Djerba, the last book he'd read, his last year at school...He explained that he had taken his *baccalauréat* last year but didn't pass. Obviously, it was a total nightmare for his mom, much more than for him. That **** (I'm censoring myself again) told him he was spending too much time at my house, and he was helping me out too often, as if to say that's what stopped him from doing his own work and studying for his exams. So it's my fault now?

Yeah, we really talked about everything. Even about...that thing that still made me a little ashamed. You know.

Nabil said he was sorry he kissed me without asking and that he hoped it hadn't upset me too much. I said no. So he started again. Except this time it was better, more skilled, like he knew what he was doing. He must have been practicing at his vacation club in Djerba with some seventeen-year-old German girl, a tourist over there with her journalist parents who work for the Bavarian tabloids. She was probably blond with green eyes, was named Petra, and had big boobs.

Anyway, he didn't jet afterward. We watched TV, him and me, and kept talking. He even stroked my hair (luckily I hadn't put on any Zit Zitoun this time). I told him lots of things about me, my family, and other stuff he didn't know...I told him about

Hamoudi, my memories of him reciting Rimbaud's poems in the hallway of number 32, and that's when Nabil caught me by surprise again. He starts giving up "The Orphans' New Year Gift" by heart and he didn't even stop as often as Hamoudi, no, he was really belting that poem out. It was beautiful. Except at the end, he kind of ruined it all because he looked at me with this sly smile and went: "Impressed, huh?" I said no, and he laughed. There you go, I made up with Nabil and I think also...I really like him. Wednesday, he's supposed to take me to the movies. I'm too happy. Last time I went to the movies, it was with school to see *The Lion King*.

I also ran into Hamoudi, Lila, and Sarah again this weekend. I was going to the shopping center for Mom when they honked their horn at me. It took me a minute to turn around and realize it was meant for me. Normally I never turn around when I hear a horn or someone whistling because it's always for the fat tramp behind me in her short candy pink top and tight jeans. Except, this time, there wasn't any other fool there. So I got in and went to the shopping center with them.

They were reeking of family bliss. I realized that this is the best thing to happen to Hamoudi since I've known him. I also noticed Hamoudi's changed cars again. This time it's a red Opel Vectra. Exactly the same as the one that social worker had jacked from the parking lot below our apartment. But OK, I'm not asking any questions.

Speaking of Cyborg Services, she's been transferred down to La Vendée, down on the west coast, because Mme DuThingamajig's back from her maternity leave. She finally gave birth to her shrimp. Of course, when she came back to see us, DuGizmo had gone to all the trouble of bringing baby photos. So we had the good fortune of seeing Lindsay (that's what she named her... no comment) still covered in placenta in her mom's arms (don't know how DuWhatchamacallit managed it, but her blowout was still looking perfect after the birth), Lindsay in the bath, Lindsay with her dad on the Ikea sofa, Lindsay going to beddie-bye in her cradle... Lindsay at the Pecaros, Lindsay in Tibet, and finally Lindsay and the Castafiore jewels. Our mannequinesque social worker looked pleased to pieces with her little Lindsay, already right on track to star in the Pampers ads in a few months...

Mme DuThingy noticed a "definite change" at our house. She said she'd try and squeeze a little more money out of social services so we can go on vacation next summer, maybe to the sea. Well...I was amazed. Maybe Mme DuWhoozit's actually the sister of Mother Teresa and Abbé Pierre and Sister Emmanuelle, she's generosity made flesh...Suddenly, I liked our dear beloved social worker. The seaside! If this isn't the best thing...I take back everything I said about you, your husband, and your baby DuThingy. I'm sorry. Maybe you're a nice chick after all.

So, anyway, to get back to Hamoudi and Lila, while we were out shopping together, they talked to me again about getting married. They both want a traditional wedding. It's weird, I wasn't expecting that from them. But at least Lila's parents will be pleased. She told me how she'd made up with them just a few days back, after they hadn't spoken for five years, in fact not since the day Lila decided to marry Sarah's dad. Hamoudi's mom, she's shouting from the top of all the towers in the neighborhood that her youngest son's getting married. According to Rachida (always a reliable source), lots of people are viewing the marriage badly because Lila's a divorcée and she already has a child by a full-blooded, born and bred French guy. But the soon-to-be newlyweds, they don't give a shit. And that's the point.

while Lila was trying on shoes in André, that cheesy shoe store where everything's fake leather, I gave Hamoudi the lowdown on Nabil. He looked really happy for me, like something amazing had happened. I was hoping he'd react that way. I know him super well, and Hamoudi's not the type to jump to conclusions and think if a girl's seeing a boy, it makes her a ****. Well, you know what I want to say...

"So you want to beat us and get married first? Is he good-looking, this Nabil of yours? I'd recognize him, if he grew up around here, right?"

"He's got big ears but he's very nice and smart and..."

"Oh! That's it, so it begins...It's over, no more 'kif-kif tomorrow' like you used to say to me all the time?"

It's true. I had nearly forgotten. But Hamoudi remembered. When he said that, it made me get crazy close to breaking down in tears. It's what I used to say all the time when I was down, and Mom and me were suddenly all on our own: "kif-kif tomorrow," same shit, different day.

But now I'd write it differently. Spell it "kiffe kiffe tomorrow," borrow from that verb *kiffer,* for when you really like something or someone. Oh yeah. That one's all mine. (That's the kind of thing Nabil would say.)

Maybe they're right, those people who say all the time that the wheel keeps turning. Maybe the effin' wheel really does turn. And maybe it's not such a big deal if Jarod from *The Pretender* is gay, because Nabil told me Rimbaud was too...And it's not important if I don't have my father anymore, because there are lots of people out there who don't have fathers. And, anyway, I have a mother...

And she's doing better. She's free, literate (or nearly), and she didn't even need therapy to get it all